Cherish Desire Singles:

Lust And Dildos

The Complete Six Part Series

featuring May

Written by

Max D

brought to you by Cherish Desire

DEDICATION

This book is dedicated to Michelle and Brute.

I hope you found your happy ending and Brute got lots of treats.

CONTENTS

Erotic Themes

This book is intended for mature audiences. Cherish Desire books contain erotica adventures featuring intense sexual situations including alternative lifestyles, perverse pleasures, and supernatural lust.

"Lust And Dildos 1 (A May Story)" themes: MF, Female Masturbation, Fingering & Implied Fisting, Dildo Play & Wearing, Vaginal & Anal Penetration, Implied Vaginal & Anal Sex, Implied Exhibitionism (Photo, Video)

"Lust And Dildos 2 (A May Story)" themes: Female Masturbation, Dildo Play & Wearing, Vaginal & Anal Penetration, Double Penetration, Implied MF, FF, Implied Canine

"Lust And Dildos 3 (A May Story)" themes: Female Masturbation, Dildo Play & Wearing, Vaginal & Anal Penetration, Fingering & Fisting, FF, Exhibitionism (Photo), Implied D/s

"Lust And Dildos 4 (A May Story)" themes: MF, D/s, Fingering & Fisting, Vaginal & Anal Penetration, Double Penetration, Stretching, Canine, Implied FF, Strap-On Sex

"Lust And Dildos 5 (A May Story)" themes: MF, FF, Dildo Play & Wearing, BDSM, D/s, Strap-On Sex, Stretching, Double Penetration, Vaginal & Anal Penetration, Implied Fisting

"Lust And Dildos 6 (A May Story)" themes: FF, Strap-On Sex, Dildo Play & Wearing, Spanking, D/s, Exhibitionism (Public), Implied MF, Implied Exhibitionism (Video)

"Lust And Dildos 1 (A May Story)"
written by Max D

Featuring May, Nicole, and Max

"Lust And Dildos 1 (A May Story)" themes: MF, Female Masturbation, Fingering & Implied Fisting, Dildo Play & Wearing, Vaginal & Anal Penetration, Implied Vaginal & Anal Sex, Implied Exhibitionism (Photo, Video)

"Sorry," May said regrettably to her co-worker on the phone, "I'm still kicking this flu bug. Don't want to get you sick." Her excuse had held for three nights in a row, but there was no way she'd get out of girl's night out on Thursday. "Plus I want to be rested up for tomorrow night. We've got three pubs to hit, and I know that I need to be in top form."

"You got that right, girlie," Nicole was disappointed but going with the flow. She was continually being brushed off by her best friend lately, but she'd find out why in time. May was terrible at keeping secrets, and eventually her latest fling would come out of the wash. "Well, take all your vitamins and drink lots of lemonade." Nicole hesitated to see if May would volunteer a secondary excuse, but her friend said nothing more. "Right. I'll message you whether the movie was any good. Bye byes."

May was grateful to whisper her goodbye. Nicole had called her right in the middle of her quiet time for writing to Max, and it was hard enough getting her thoughts organized and written down. Interruptions were train wrecks, but to not answer Nicole's call would have been an invite for her friend to swing by. May walked around her living room and kitchen, got a fresh cup of sweet tea from the fridge, and then put her phone on silent and plugged it in to charge. She was tempted to procrastinate some more, but she only had an hour or two before Max would call. He'd upped the incentives for her story writing - as well as the suggested punishments to push her past her writer's block.

As soon as she sat down, May's German Shepherd whined softly for attention. "Oh, sheesh," she muttered. "Come over here, you big lug. But you are not featuring in this story. No matter how much Max would like that!" He perked his ears and got up with a tongue lolling smile. "Come on, bright boy. Come sit by the couch with me." He didn't need a second invitation. Tail slightly wagging, he lumbered over to the couch and slid heavily to the floor. His wet nose nudged at her arm, and May reached over and petted the top of his head while re-reading her story so far.

It wasn't very good. She knew it. Max would

know it. But it was a start, and he kept encouraging her to just write rather than criticize. She went back to her outline guide. The story was supposed to be a simple short about a woman playing with her butt plug. Somehow it had gotten off track talking about clothes and shoes and candles and ambience. May suspected Max only cared about the action scenes. All the description and storytelling was simply a mechanism to avoid getting explicit. There was no way that she was going to avoid his punishment tonight.

She sighed and Brute let out a heavy breath in response while lowering his long snout to rest on the cool floor. "Oh, it's not like you're going to have to suffer," she murmured to her big overgrown dog. "I'm the one whose ass is on the line... literally," but she knew what he was getting at. Her big boy thought he was still a puppy and liked cuddling on her chest at night, so Max's late evening calls cut into his mom time. "It won't be so bad, big boy. Just a bit of patience. I'll figure this out somehow." May wasn't sure if she was referring to Max or the writing or both.

~~~

"Thanks for sending over a draft," Max was calm and reserved. "Looks like you had some good ideas but kept going off in random directions." Maybe he was tired; May couldn't tell for sure. "Would you like some suggestions?"
~~~

She got the hardest part out of the way right up front. "I know I didn't finish it. I tried to avoid any distractions, but I'm not used to sitting down and focusing on writing. You've been doing this for such a long time after all." May supposed that he didn't respond because she hadn't answered his question. "So, yes, I could use some suggestions. But, ummm, I already have the new big plug in my bottom so hopefully that helps." As soon as she'd sent him her very rough and incomplete story, May had lubed her bottom and sat on the three inch wide red anal plug until it went into her ass. She knew Max deserved a reward for his effort even if she really was trying hard to do something that they both knew wasn't her forte.

Max took a deep breath. "Wow. Well, that's some great initiative." If writing poorly meant May was willing to push her limits then maybe this wasn't as bad as it seemed. "When I said I'd like you to write a story, maybe you thought it had to be hardcore porn or something. If writing about something sexy without the sex scenes is easier-"

"It's ok, Max," she cut him off gently. "I know what you want. You sent me a lot of good ideas. I just, well, I don't know how to write it." It wasn't his fault that she sucked at this. No one had ever asked her to tell sexy stories before.

Nodding, he took a step back. "I'm going to send you a set of stories by a handful of authors. Each has a slightly different style and different way of describing things. Go ahead and read them, think about how they are putting together their scenes, and go from there. But ultimately this comes down to

"Lust And Dildos 1 (A May Story)"

advice I always try to remember: Go forth with no limits, no inhibitions, and no expectations. Some stories tell themselves. They can't be corralled and organized by an outline. Explore your characters. You wrote about this woman's shoe collection. It says something about her. Each pair of shoes is a memory of a man or a place or a party. Tell those stories. Whatever they may be." He left it at that. The creative process wasn't something that could be forced. Either May stumbled into her own passions or she would continue to wander in the shallow end of her potential.

It was so different hearing him talk about writing. It sounded so easy, but, in practice, May couldn't seem to get it right. "Can we talk about something else? I'm already disappointed in myself." She was just being honest even though it hurt to admit her failings. "I didn't have any problems with the plug. I guess I was expecting it to be much worse than it really is."

"Didn't have any problems? I would have thought there'd be more stretching before you could handle something that wide. Pretty impressive if you just rode it until it slipped inside." He moved to a new topic without resistance. May would sort out her other issues in time.

"Well, I had to wiggle a lot, and I definitely felt it drag my butt in with it. But the lube worked well, and I've been practicing with my beige plug for two days straight. This one felt wider, but it doesn't stab as deep. I thought you'd like to know I took some photos, too. With your name and a little heart on my butt." She laughed and the plug felt solid within her bottom while her belly shook. "Of course, no one else can read my handwriting, but it sort of looks like your name and a heart..."

Max smiled. "Bit of a reach around. Maybe I should have a little rubber stamp made. Then you could just mark my name wherever you wanted." He chuckled to himself.

"Ok," May replied seriously. "I could do that. I wonder if Michaels has one I can buy already made." The quiet on the other end of the phone made her wonder what she'd said wrong. "Max? Is that alright?"

"It's a good story idea. Going out to the store, sifting through the shelves, finally finding the stamp and picking out ink pads. All while wearing your plug in your bottom, the thin handle poking at your labia and tailbone, and feeling it move when you sit and stand and drive. Cleaning up when you get home - wiping off everything with wet wipes and then toweling off. The stain of the ink sinking into your pale skin and blurring on the edges as you lift the rubber stamp away. Posing for photos, making sure your ass is on display. Would you sleep with the plug in and my name still stamped on your bottom? What kind of dreams do you have when Brute curls up next to you and leans against your bare breasts while your cheeks are partially spread by the plug's base?"

For him it came so easily, and May listened to his spontaneous storyline wondering how she could ever

"Lust And Dildos 1 (A May Story)"

even get one thing written. "I should get a bigger plug," she admitted quietly. "Every week I can't produce a story, I will need something slightly deeper or slightly wider." She sighed as her German Shepherd nosed around her calves while preparing to leap into bed with her. "Brute apparently likes the idea. He always comes close now to hear your voice, you know."

Max didn't press her buttons. He could tell that she was frustrated, and sexual innuendo about her lusty canine wasn't a good way to help her relax. "Is that your story then?" he was deliberately hopeful. "The story of a sexy girl who pushes herself to write an erotic story for her friend or face the consequences of a bigger and longer sex toy in her bottom? I like it." His supportive tone fit with his words. "Maybe what you need is less of an outline and more of a play by play. Break it down into steps. Then you can expand on those based on your experience and what you've heard and read." Every writer was different so Max tried to offer a variety of different approaches.

"Oh, I don't know. I got undressed. I used the toilet and rinsed off in the shower. I used two fingers to lube my bottom while leaning into my pillows. I moved to sit on the plug. I wiggled and pushed and let my body sink onto it. It went in, that last bit pulling my ass with it until the wider base popped through my opening. Now, I'm wearing it." She was used to describing how she played with herself. Max had been encouraging her to share things like that for a few months already.

"There you go. You've already got a handle on it. Now the question you have to ask yourself is 'why.' Why does she just use two fingers? Why does she leave the bathroom and stretch out in bed? Why does she push herself?" He was being too cerebral, but it was exciting to see the pieces fit together. "Why are you wearing a plug right now?"

A stroke of lightning shook May enough that Brute stopped and stared up at her with his deep dark eyes. "That's what this is about?" She thought about it: the stories, the options, the sexual play between them. "You want to know 'why?'" It seemed so obvious, but it led to a runaway train of scattered thoughts. "You want to know what I like. You want to know how I see things. You want to know what I pay attention to." When Max didn't reply, May whispered, "I have a plug in my ass because it pleases you."

He whispered back, "I know. But I don't know what else you might try." Max didn't correct May's intuition. Maybe it was accurate, and Max hadn't thought about things that way. "Why a bigger plug each week? Soon the plugs will be too huge and painful for you."

"I'm not afraid of a little pain," she teased Max and realized that a weight had been lifted off her shoulders. "I guess I should write down my reasons. I'll give it another try. Maybe I can have something for you tomorrow night before I go out with Nicole."

"That would be great. Of course, if you don't get it done then I guess wearing your plug for the evening might be a good reminder." Max tested the waters carefully because he didn't know exactly what Nicole thought of May keeping in touch with him.

Blushing so hard that her cheeks were burning, May dropped her phone and had to fumble for it while Brute chose that moment to launch himself into bed with her. "Sorry... sorry... sorry..." she repeated while trying to grab her cell without accidentally hanging up. Brute nosed around and tried to curl up on her thighs while May was distracted, and she had to both rescue her phone and prevent her big baby from crushing her with his bulk. "Ok... got it... hold on... Brute! Move!" Max was laughing when May finally got her phone to her ear. "What? Don't make me yell at you, too."

Still smirking and knowing that May could hear his amusement in his voice, Max replied, "I'll take that as a 'yes.' Plug stays in for four hours each night until the story is done. Sounds swell." He waited for her retort.

Struggling to get Brute settled, May was exasperated when she replied, "I can't do that. I want to, but what if I need a bathroom break or something? I can't-" She was cut off by Max's quiet command.

"You will do it. Unless you have a much better excuse anyway. How can you move to a bigger plug each week if you can't even wear this plug each evening? I'm trying to help you and save you some discomfort." He was being infuriatingly rational, and they both knew it.

Knowing better than to risk exposing the secrets that she kept from Nicole, May had to agree. "Ok. But if it doesn't work out then I don't want you disappointed. I'll start out with it in, but no promises." She took a breath while her German Shepherd slumped into her ribs and kicked his feet to firmly plant himself against her side. "Brute is quite comfortably snuggled in next to me now, so I should probably get going, Max. Thanks for the suggestions and, ummm, help." She was ready to hang up and turn off the light, but Max said something and she had to put her phone back to her ear. "What was that?"

"Aren't you forgetting something?" he was grinning from ear to ear while blowing her a kiss.

Flustered and unsure what Max was on about, May whispered, "Good night, you crazy man." She hung up before he could object and then tried to get comfortable.

It was a good fifteen minutes before May realized that Max was probably alluding to the fact that she still had her three inch wide butt plug buried in her bottom, but that was ok. If she could sleep with it in then four hours the next evening would be a piece of cake.

~~~

Her email began, "Here's my special story just for
~~~

"Lust And Dildos 1 (A May Story)"

you, Max." There was no title or prelude. May launched into the details right away, almost like she was afraid to describe the scene because then she'd get off topic and lost in the words.

|~|~|~|~|~|~|

She slept with his big plug in her bottom. She didn't wonder why or ponder the meaning of doing so. She just did it. Her ass would clench now and again, and the stretched pucker of her asshole burned slightly. She remained as still as she could and worried about cramping that never really came. In the darkness, the sensations coming from her bottom and her vagina were the only things that seemed real. There was no denying the slick moisture that kept her pussy lips damp and made her buttocks feel slimy. There was no question that her body was passively aroused as if she was waiting for a lover to slip into bed and spread her thighs at any moment.

That thought led to others. What would happen if he were here? Could he push his cock into her pussy alongside the broad base of the anal plug in her ass? He would, she decided. He wouldn't just try. He would keep going, prying her slick labia apart and pressing his rigid cock against her opening until he was inside of her. She could imagine his heat and pride, the look of joy in his eyes, but something was missing. Her fingers dabbed at the rivulets of juice clinging to her fleshy swollen lips. She slipped a fingertip between her pink folds, breaking the weeping seal, and her fingers followed.

In her dark bedroom, the soft moans of her pleasure mingled with the sweet scent of her sex. Two of her fingers probed her opening, feeling the hard edge of the butt plug pressing upward into her pussy, and slipping past it to stroke her inner walls. She was so very wet and tender. There was a flash flood of warm juices flowing out along the length of her fingers, and every time she pushed in deeper, more came out and wet her hand and lips. She imagined that she was drilling into herself, drilling for oil, and unleashed a spouting gusher when her fingers came out and she deliberately clenched her vaginal muscles.

The plug in her ass had felt so big when she'd sat on it earlier in the evening. Now the easy passage her fingers found into her hollow pussy made it seem like the plug was far too small. It didn't make any sense logically. The three inch wide base was the biggest thing that she had ever fucked. It even looked big next to her other sex toys. But her sense of touch didn't lie. Her two fingers plunged into her pussy again, easily sliding past her soaked inner labia, and she was convinced that a wider plug was both possible and necessary.

That made her pause. Necessary? What was she really trying to achieve? She wanted him to know, to appreciate, how she fucked herself for him. She wanted to show off how her body looked - including the intimate details of her pretty pussy and plugged bottom. But where did this specific urge come from? Why was it so important to completely stuff her ass for him? Her hand pressed into her clit while her fingers slipped deeper as they sought out her g-spot. It felt too good for her to allow her worried thoughts ruin the pleasure.

Aware of the growing wet spot between her buttocks and soaking her sheets, her fingers stroked in and out while the plug surfed the bobbing waves of her clenching inner walls. She found her g-spot, high up and in a hollow cavern within her sex that was so empty compared to the tightness near her opening. Maybe that was the problem. She was distracted by the buzz of her impending release, but the back of her mind was still worrying over the little details.

She tried to shut down those dubious thoughts by murmuring to herself, "Well, next time use a phallus or a full plug instead of a cone shaped toy." It didn't really help though hearing her own voice disrupted the quiet engulfing her. She felt like she had to respond - wasn't that a sure sign of insanity - so she whispered back, "A nice thick long plug - with a rounded head - like the one I saw online." It was as if she was talking with him but acting out both parts.

None of that mattered. Her visualization combined with what she could feel within her pelvis. Her fingers stroked into the hollow space within her pussy, and she imagined the wide base of the plug continuing all the way alongside her groping digits. She moaned, softly at first and then louder, while deliberately grinding her fingertips into her wet inner walls. Just like it would feel like worming her two fingers in while being squeezed forward by the thick shaft of cylindrical dildo buried in her ass.

Her pussy clenched, unhappy being hollow and anticipating something much more filling, and she regretted her heat and perverse urges while feeding her dirty fantasy with more of the same. "Just my ass," she murmured. She knew he'd love to fist her pussy. She'd even started out playing more with her vagina than her bottom. But somehow his recurring encouragement to do the same with her bottom had tipped her into focusing on much more frequent anal play. Now she imagined that it was her ass that she was giving to him, keeping her pussy for herself and her two fingers, but even while she pretended to hold to that truth, she knew that it was a blatant self-deception. He'd fucked her - vaginally and anally - and everything that she did with her toys and her own fingers encouraged more of the same.

Abs trembling, she pressed her fingers directly into her g-spot and ground her palm against her clit. The three inch wide plug made her ass ache every time she clenched down, but it seemed to be going deeper as well. She didn't care anymore. She just wanted to orgasm, to get off, and then to fall asleep in her own wet spot. Selfish self love. Saying that it was for him was just an excuse to masturbate more often and enjoy the endorphin

"Lust And Dildos 1 (A May Story)"

rush.

Or was it? Her orgasm came and rolled through her abdomen accompanied by ragged gasps and kicking legs. The muscles of her thighs and lower back ached while her body arched and her fingernails clawed at her inner walls. When she settled back into bed, the sheets were moist with her perspiration. It didn't matter, she tried to tell herself. She could sleep like this. But the darkness and endorphins weren't enough.

Eyes closed, she imagined how the big rounded head of the new plug would feel wedged between her petite buttocks and painfully tugging her asshole open. There was more wetness seeping from her pussy, and the cleft of her ass and around the base of the plug was already uncomfortably soaked in her juices. She imagined what it would look like and tried to figure out in her head how to position the camera to make a video of the broad shaft penetrating her. Even trying to divert into technical details like setting up her room for the video and making sure that she looked clean wasn't enough.

Her fingers found her pussy lips, splayed and coated with tacky juices on the edges while fresh wetness filled the inner folds, and her two fingers plunged into her sex again. It was going to be a long night, but she was determined to sleep with the plug in her bottom. Masturbating would eventually tire her out. Right?

|~|~|~|~|~|~|

Max read the short story twice, and then sent back some simple suggestions.   He liked how May communicated what the main character was feeling. He liked the casual interaction with the reader. He wondered what she looked like.

He fully expected May's response to be, "She looks like me."

"Lust And Dildos 2 (A May Story)"

written by Max D

Featuring May, Nicole, and Max

"Lust And Dildos 2 (A May Story)" themes: Female Masturbation, Dildo Play & Wearing, Vaginal & Anal Penetration, Double Penetration, Implied MF, FF, Implied Canine

Still certain that May was holding out on her, Nicole was forced to be gentle to her best friend. "You look utterly wiped out," she squeezed May's hand and felt the weakness in her response. "Were you really that sick this week?"

Struggling on just a few hours of sleep, May nodded. She'd been a zombie all day. The only brief moments of real awareness had come when it was time to take out the three inch wide plug in her bottom. It pulled and stretched her ass so much - the wide base straining her sphincter while she yanked on the small handle - that May had almost given up.

Only her steadfast need to use the potty had urged her on. In the hot shower, her ass had finally spread enough to let the red butt plug pop free. It hurt so bad that May coasted on a surge of adrenaline while washing up. That didn't stop her from relubing her bottom after work and sitting on the plug again. Even if she'd managed to send Max a short story that he would like.

"Ok, we got to get our game faces on." Nicole tried to rally her girlfriend into action, but there wasn't a lot to work with. "Three pubs, plenty of Irish boys, and a chance for you to finally get some action! We need to make sure this isn't just beer going to waste." May gave her a squeamish look, and Nicole shook her head. "Oh, no, you don't. I expect you to at least manage a pint at each pub. It'll make you feel better."

But May knew the truth. Her pussy ached from being fingered. Her ass was sore and uncomfortable with her plug in. The last thing she wanted or needed was to get drunk and hook up with one of Nicole's firehouse boys. "Beer, yes," she sighed. "But I'm in no shape for a wild romp." She didn't put her foot down too hard because Nicole would take that as a challenge.

"Not even a 'pressed against an alley wall while he pounds your ass' kind of quickie?" Nicole laughed when May turned slightly green. "Ha! Ok, you've been ill so I guess all the good fun stuff is out. Hope you don't mind if I get my licks in though. I've been horny for two weeks straight."

"Lust And Dildos 2 (A May Story)"

"I could tell," May smiled. "Ok, let's do this thing." She fussed with her pleated skirt and fluffed her hair in the mirror of Nicole's pickup truck. "Two girls, three pubs, and I promise to try not to yawn too often."

"That's the spirit! Keep your eyes forward and lead with your chin."

~~~

Max listened while May's voice slipped from a whisper into a murmur. Not everything she said was making it across the connection, but he understood she was exhausted and had tried to get her to go to sleep several times. The alcohol was keeping her mumbling along, meandering while trying to connect with him, and Max kept her company because he sensed that she needed someone there to hear her out.

"So I'll remember next time... width, length, and penetration. Got to get those right. I mean, I can always feel your plug fucking my ass. But I don't know how deep my fingers go. I should measure them, but it's probably only a few inches. Maybe it's more than that, but I always curl my fingertips to dig into my spot so maybe it's less. I don't know. I came like a dozen times last night... never done that before. Tonight, I've still got that red plug in my ass - the one we were looking at online together. It's definitely closer to three inches wide, but maybe only four
~~~

inches deep. How's that possible? How can it be so wide but not very long? I think I need something more rounded at the top and thicker. Definitely thicker. My fingers move too easily inside of me. Something thicker would fill me up better..."

Max injected "Sure" and "Of course" and "Uh-huh" in the right spots. May kept rambling. Finally he'd hit his time limit, but he didn't want to leave May hanging. "Sexy," he interrupted her stream of consciousness, "I want to hear you fucking your pussy with that thick plug. Then I can link you to some thicker and longer toys." He meant at some point in the future, but May took everything very literally.

"What? Oh, sure... I need to wash it off first. Hold on." Her phone was fumbled into the bed sheets and comforter, and Max listened to Brute's heavy breathing while the German Shephard sniffed at the handset. May vanished for long minutes, and Max rested his eyes with his cell phone propped against the side of his head. She was talking to herself from a distance about fifteen minutes later, and Max laughed when he heard her exclaim, "Oh, you big pretty boy. Whatcha got there? Oh, you. Stealing mommy's phone. Don't... ugh... licking my face... oh, you! Wait. Stop. Sit down." The muffled sounds of May and Brute suddenly became crisp and clear. Max suspected May had just scooped her phone off the bed. "Hello? Is someone there?"

"Just me, May," Max said quietly. "Hanging out with Brute."

"Lust And Dildos 2 (A May Story)"

She must have shoo'd Brute out of her room because there was a heavy thud followed by a scurrying noise and then the sound of a door shutting. "Oh, I'm so sorry, Max. I needed a bathroom break. Give me a minute." The phone line went dead.

Sighing while stretching out across the hotel bed, Max waited for the call back that he hadn't asked for in the first place. Now he needed to rest, and May was likely to fall asleep as soon as she turned out the lights in her room. His phone buzzed and he answered, "Hello there." He didn't expect her semi alert state to last long.

May nervously sucked on her lower lip while settling into her pillows. "Sorry about that. I've been pretty tired. I should probably get some sleep." Her voice began to droop, and Max was sure she'd turned out the lights and was curling up next to Brute.

"Ok, sleep well then." Max was ready to go, too.

Feeling her second wind blow out like a candle in a rainstorm, May was tempted to just hang up. But she knew that she'd promised something and despite the rapid lethargy wrapping around her body, she wanted to make sure Max understood her commitment. "I'll try wearing the plug in my pussy tomorrow. Four hours. It helps me think and write better." She blew a kiss to him and yawned loudly. "And then I'll take some more photos, just for you, and try to make a video of my pussy and bottom being fucked." Brute grunted and pressed into her ribs, his big head tipped back against her breast. "Sorry... so sleepy all of a sudden."

Max laughed. His bones ached and his hotel room had an odd smell of chemical cleanser. "Me, too. Give Brute a goodnight kiss." He could hear the big German Shepherd moving around.

Smiling, May said, "He's a good boy. He keeps playing with my nipples because he thinks he might get some milk from them." She sighed and wiggled to her left to escape Brute's attempt to roll over on top of her. "Dumb but sweet."

Struggling to sound as interested as he would have been if this topic had come up an hour before, Max asked, "Why so much attention to your nips? Feeling swollen?" He knew if he stayed up much longer then he wouldn't sleep at all.

"I'll write you about it," May sighed happily. "Can't keep my eyes open."

~~~

He was surprised to see that May was willing to indulge him so much when he had a chance to read her latest attempt at a sexy story. Max sent her an email before finishing it, just to encourage May, and then took a dinner break before opening it up again.

His phone buzzed. "You liked it? ;)" Her short text message was a hint that May was out with Nicole.
~~~

"Lust And Dildos 2 (A May Story)"

"Of course. You knew I would."

"Gotta go. Trying something new. Might need to pee a lot."

Max pondered the possibilities before replying. "Bigger?"

Blushing and hiding her phone from Nicole while riding the Metro into the city, May texted back, "Two toys both ends." Then she deleted the text message thread and stuffed her phone back in her pocket.

"Who was that?" Nicole asked. She'd seen May's furtive attempt to disguise what she was doing.

May knew she couldn't get away with saying it was no one. "A boy," she replied carefully. She anticipated Nicole grabbing for her phone. "I deleted it already."

Her best friend glared at her. "A boy that you don't want me to know about? How interesting." Nicole sized up May's resistance. "No wonder someone was sick all week. Boy cooties!"

She wasn't about to admit the cause of her exhaustion was too much masturbation and frequent late night calls with Max, but Nicole would press harder if May didn't tell her something. "He's long distance." She sighed and frowned. "And you wouldn't like him."

"And why is that? I love bad boys. Is he one of your puritanical right wing types? Again?" Nicole squinted at May and stabbed upward with her right hand. "Is he invested by the power of the holy spirit to penetrate you? Tell me!"

May laughed. "He's older than you like. Must be my recurring sugar daddy complex." The two plugs secretly rocking within her pelvis moved with her belly and distracted May for a moment. "But I was wiped out. He's been so nice sending me little text messages and calling to check up on me. Not like my best friend who keeps demanding I come out to help her pickup dirty boy toys." She matched Nicole's stare and then they both broke out in peals of laughter.

People looked around at them and then quickly looked back. They'd be partially right assuming that the two well dressed young women had been pre-drinking, but Nicole never missed a chance to mock an audience. She took May's hand and tugged her into a warm embrace. "You and me before boys," she whispered to her girlfriend's ear. "You know you're terrible when it comes to keeping secrets." Her little love bite on May's ear emphasized her dominance and implied intimacy to the onlookers.

Squirming free, May pretended to be offended. "How dare you? On our first date? In public!" Now heads turned but not all whipped back when May stared back at them. A few men and women continued to look over the two women. "I hope you understand my father won't approve of such scandalous behaviour." She mock pouted for the audience, and then leaned in close to Nicole's lips. "Just be gentle... I'm a virgin." Her mocking stage

"Lust And Dildos 2 (A May Story)"

whisper triggered a few groans and one woman clucked her tongue.

"Oh, that's ok," Nicole said brightly. "I've got lots of experience." Her laugh broke the tension on the train car, and May and Nicole's mock drama scene was over. They went back to talking about Nicole's work week, and May enjoyed the shuddering vibrations of the Metro car moving the two vinyl dildos inside of her pussy and ass.

~~~

Before you ask, he's too small for me. Poor Brute, he's such a beauty, but he's not much when it comes to down there. My nipples have been swollen and chaffed for days now. His rough tongue is no relief, but the texture difference gives me goose bumps. I tried stopping him, but he paws at my bedroom door whenever I'm masturbating now. He thinks I'm moaning because I'm hurt. And maybe I am, a little bit, because my pussy and ass are so sore every day now.

That's probably why my nipples are so tender and full. I'm turned on for hours of the day, unable to do anything about it, and everything seems to rub against the most sensitive spots. Whether I wear thongs or panties doesn't matter.
~~~

The fabric pulls on my lips and gets wet and sticky. The bits flossing my ass and stroking over my labia rub me raw, and I have to fight the urge to walk with my thighs apart. At the same time, I'm always unconsciously clenching. The plugs inside of me move with my body so squeezing down helps hold them in place. But you can only grip them for so long before giving yourself a tummy ache. So I have to take deep breaths and let the sex toys float inside of me from time to time.

My brave and trusty, Brute. He just wants to save his mommy from whatever is bothering her. He wants to give me kisses and steps onto my belly while I'm writhing from the intensity of being double penetrated as I pinch my clit. He wants to calm me down, curling up on my chest like when he was a little puppy to let me know he's there to comfort me. He's so sweet when he rubs his wet nose against my cheeks and licks my ears. All while I'm crushed beneath the bulk of his furry body and orgasming with two plugs rubbing against each other within my sex and bottom.

I know what you'd wonder. You're such a dirty old man. But like I said, he's just too small. And cut. He wouldn't know what to do if he even had it in him. Brute's a cuddler and maybe a licking demon, but not lover or fighter. I usually manage to slide him off to the side, and he whimpers now and again when I arch my back and orgasm for a second and third time, but only because he wants me to know he cares. He doesn't understand. It's my fault that he's upset. My lust that keeps pushing me on. I'd blame you, but it's definitely

"Lust And Dildos 2 (A May Story)"

me. Though if you were here...

Think about that. Think about it while you watch the short videos I share of my ass slowly spreading and the thick anal plug popping inside of me. Think about it while you watch the longer clip of me pushing and pulling the base of the same three inch wide plug in and out of my slick pussy. Think about it when I send you links to the bigger toys I'd like to have. I need something bigger and longer to fill the hollows my fingers can feel inside of me. I need something between my cheeks that I shouldn't even want spreading my labia. Need. Want. Same thing really.

What would you do if you were here? What if it was you coming into my bedroom instead of my precious, Brute? Would you lick and suckle my breasts and nipples? Would you kiss my ears and whisper to me with heated breath? Would you help me? Would you let me rest with one hand settled on your side while you do the hard work? Would you piston those sex toys in and out of me over and over again?

Would you, Max? Because I think that's what I need.

| ~ | ~ | ~ | ~ | ~ |

May finished writing in a rush. Max was right about one thing: Once a story started flowing, it took on a life of its own. There was no doubt in her mind that she hadn't anticipated the ending. It was a surprise for her, but May was sure Max would enjoy it thoroughly. She skimmed the text for errors, hoping to catch any obvious mistakes, but gave up as soon as she got past the first couple of paragraphs.

She needed some hot tea and a bathroom break. Maybe a long hot shower and soak. Her poor pussy felt tender and bruised, and her ass hurt even when she was standing still or resting on her side in bed. Her playful night out with Nicole was meant to last a few hours, but May didn't get home until four in the morning. Dancing, drinking, trying to pee around the plugs, and then the same all over again - for over six hours. The road had seemed like it would go on forever when May was finally driving the last thirty minutes back to her place. At least she'd been able to finally spread her feet wide enough to let her swollen pussy lips hang low between her inner thighs without being squeezed together.

And now the question came to her again. How much was too much? Sure, May was having fun or she wouldn't be playing with herself. But six days of wearing something inside of her bottom, pussy, or both was pretty crazy. May decided it was like going to the gym: a break every three days for a day was probably ideal. But the urge to keep going, to see how long she could last, was hard to resist.

Maybe just one plug at a time, except for special occasions, wouldn't feel so bad. May thought about that some more and decided it would need to be a bigger sex toy just to keep things challenging. She definitely blamed Max for that thought. He'd teased her, suggesting she was just some vanilla girl who read about boys in Cosmo, and May knew that had fired up her competitive spirit. She also knew keeping her dildo adventures secret from Nicole was making things more exciting. They'd been dirty dancing on the dance floor, and Nicole didn't even know that she was grinding her thigh into the base of a plug in May's pussy.

She blushed. Nicole would die when she found out that she had unknowingly been fucking May. It seemed so wrong, but that was the sort of trump card May could use over and over again. Next time Nicole was all like, "I want the tall sexy guy, you deal with his lumpy friend," May could coyly reply, "Remember when you fucked me and didn't even know it?" End of conversation. Nicole would be so flustered that she'd fail to make a witty retort for hours.

A hot shower and maybe cleaning everything out was a good plan. May got out of bed and Brute fell into step alongside her. The big dog was still convinced that she needed to be taken care of and rarely let her out of his sight in the evenings. May patted his solid head and walked into the bathroom. As soon as the water was hot, she'd take the plugs out. Or maybe after soaking for a bit so she wouldn't be so sore. She grabbed some lube and stripped out of her pajamas. Bent over in front of her shower tub to test the water temperature, May had to swat Brute's nose away from her bottom as he curiously sniffed at her lady scent. To her surprise, he pushed forward anyway, and May almost fell into the tub when his cold wet nose pushed into the cleft of her ass and his rough tongue licked her spread labia and the base of the plugs.

"Brute! Damn you! Don't let Max give you ideas." May stumbled forward, caught herself on the wall of the shower, and then almost tumbled over the edge of the bath. Her obvious displeasure made Brute back away and whimper while sitting by the toilet. "Sorry, buddy," May consoled him gently once she was straightened out and not at risk of falling down. "Got to have some limits." His big pleading eyes didn't understand. "And you don't want a bath, do you?"

Bath was something Brute understood very well. He got up and moved to the bathroom door and curled up on the floor as far from the tub as possible. "Didn't think so, mister." May sighed and got into the shower. It was warm and soothing, but her heart was still pounding from the shock her big German Shepherd - or rather his tongue - had given her. "Damn, Max... giving innocent Brute ideas..." she muttered and then got into the hot water and pulled the beige shower curtain shut.

"Lust And Dildos 3 (A May Story)"
written by Max D

Featuring May, Nicole, and Max

"Lust And Dildos 3 (A May Story)" themes: Female Masturbation, Dildo Play & Wearing, Vaginal & Anal Penetration, Fingering & Fisting, FF, Exhibitionism (Photo), Implied D/s

Max's gift spread her buttocks apart, stretched her tender rosebud, and drilled into her bottom. The toy was a warm copper colour and made of deceptively soft silicon material, but there was no doubting his intentions. Even if it was a reward for her short sexy stories and dedication, Max had given her the larger dildo because he wanted May to push her butt and her pussy harder.

Not that May offered any resistance. Using four fingers, she had quickly lubed up her ass and almost skipped giving the heavy dildo a thorough wash before sitting on the soft tip to see how well it would fit inside of her openings. And now that she had the thick toy inside of her, her buttocks unable to clench shut because the broad base was too solid and massive for her to do more than squeeze on the pliable shaft while shuddering, May had no intention of giving up. Her little steno pad and favorite pen were sitting on her pillow, and May rocked her hips while kneeling to best grind her bottom against the dildo. Brute came over to sniff around, but her big German Shepherd was mostly interested in finding a place to slump down near May and then sprawl out while relaxing.

Relaxing. May grinned and began scribbling down ideas. What would it feel like, to know, to be stretched and relaxing with her new massive dildo embedded in her bottom? What sorts of things did a woman do while riding a four inch thick squishy silicon dildo with her ass? Her fingers played over her exposed labia, and May realized that the hefty shaft was pushing her lips forward and outward from her smooth pelvis. She imagined the lewd and obscene display of her pussy, and May ran her tongue over her teeth and grinned. If only she dared... if only she was so bold...

May knew that she wasn't. Her hand stroked Brute's hard head while he nudged her thigh, and she reassured him that his mommy was ok even if she was moaning and sighing a lot. He'd goosed her a few times lately. Mostly out of curiosity or drawn in by the scent of her sex. Even though her shaved pussy was prominently placed on display and thrust forward from the natural curve of her pelvis, May didn't dare teach Brute to take advantage of her with his rough

"Lust And Dildos 3 (A May Story)"

tongue. It just wasn't something she would do, even if the thought of closing her eyes while something heavy and wet dragged over her labia made the blood sing in her veins.

"Maybe Max..." she pondered and went back to writing down ideas. He had been right about one thing: with her pussy or her ass plugged, she was a much more focused writer. With such an enormous toy in her ass, there didn't seem to be much more left to do though. Her notes were largely disconnected thoughts, but May kept coming back to what it might feel like and how pleasurable it would be to have something else. Something more. Something... decadent.

Eyes closed while resting, the smooth giant dildo holding her buttocks apart no matter how hard they tried to squeeze shut, May whispered, "Nicole's pretty tongue..." It was a flash of inspiration and so deliciously dirty and wrong. Her girlfriend, cohort, and nosy work buddy had been trying harder and harder to pry into May's discrete texting sessions and calls with Max. Thoughts of how Max might punish Nicole for interfering with their fun encouraged May to grind hard against the soft copper shaft in her bottom. He'd been teasing, but May was sure that Max honestly would intervene if Nicole tried to stop her from fucking dildos for him.

That was inspiration enough for her next story.

$$|\sim|\sim|\sim|\sim|\sim|$$

Her tongue caressing my poor swollen clit and tender labia in each photo, Nicole's pretty lingerie and high heels show off her sexy body while she makes me cum. The camera keeps taking pictures, continuously focusing and blinding us both with the bright flash, while she delivers her apologies one lick at a time. Even though she covers it up, I know Nicole is flushed and aroused. I can smell her sweet pussy as well as my own. I tease her about not touching herself, not giving in, and not admitting that licking me makes her dripping wet. Secretly I'm hoping the camera flash makes it clear that her black panties are soaked.

I want her exposed for the slut she is. Not the sort of brazen extroverted sexual voyeur that Nicole likes to pretend to be. I know that's all just an act to hide how she really feels. It's easier for her to flirt with a dozen guys and pick one that will just bang her for the weekend than it is for Nicole to admit what she needs. It's so much simpler for her to lie about what she's looking for and pretend friends with benefits is good enough than admit she's desperate for a man that will give her what I already have. A man who will text her dirty thoughts at work. A man who will demand that she flash her pussy at him in the movie theater. A man who will send her big dildos and ask her to write about her progress.

A man like you.

Every kiss of her soft lips tastes of my sex. She

"Lust And Dildos 3 (A May Story)"

thinks this is just about turning on my mysterious boyfriend, so she's more than willing to apologize for prying into my affair with you. Nicole is pretty smart, but for some reason she hasn't put the puzzle pieces together this time. She takes advantage of me as she always has, suddenly putting herself on top and fingering my wet pussy. More bravado and machismo. More showing off in an attempt to prove she's better than me. I know her so well that I made her trim and file her nails before coming over. If it was just for me then Nicole would have said no, but she can't resist the allure of the camera and the chance to compete for your desire.

Two fingers. Three. I'm not stopping her, but Nicole is starting to get curious and nervous. Four fingers and she's smiling to cover up how her breath is becoming rapid and shallow while her hand is trembling. "Go ahead," I whisper to her with a sly smile, "I can take more." She's trapped in her own head - struggling with what it means - and I reach down and hold her wrist while gently pushing out onto her fingers. "But if I can handle it..."

"I can do better," she mutters immediately. Oh, Nicole can't help being competitive. She's in every situation to win. "He can't like this anyway." She tries to pull her hand back, but I'm not letting go so easily. "Guys aren't into... well... you know."

"He is," I challenge her. "He totally is." She's not pulling away, but Nicole isn't committing either. "Just do me, so he can see how fucked I am, and that'll be enough for today. And stay off my phone or it'll be your turn next." She deserved worse than my pussy wrapped around her hand and my labia suckling her wrist, but I was counting on her urges to push her further than I can.

With a smirk, she drove her hand straight into my sex. No extra lube and no waiting for me to get ready. Your demands that I keep playing with my big toys daily are paying off, but I don't tell you about that. I don't want to encourage you to start dry fucking my pussy and bottom until I get soaking wet in anticipation whenever I see a dildo. For you? Me fucking for you. I do all the hard work in our relationship, and you love it.

"Dirty little slut," Nicole mutters as she sinks into my pussy with her small hand. It's meant to be demeaning, but the way her breasts are heaving under Nicole's semi-sheer black teddy gives away how turned on my girlfriend is. Practicing my kegels, clenching and unclenching on her knuckles within my pussy, it's harder and harder for her to maintain the illusion of just doing this because I asked her to.

"You remember..." I murmur while caressing her forearm. Nicole starts pushing her hand in and out, just enough to bob the widest part around the base of her hand and her thumb joint within my opening, and I have to catch my breath. I wasn't prepared for how good it feels having someone else control the sensations within my pussy. I'm so used to riding my fingers and dildos

"Lust And Dildos 3 (A May Story)"

that I forgot how someone else being in control changes everything. "...when we went out dancing and I kept needing to go to the bathroom?"

Nicole nods. She always thought that night was odd, and her curiosity with our text messages on the train ride into the city had been what led down the path to her sneaking off with my phone and trying to undelete our conversations so she could snoop on me.

"You were dancing with me... showing off to the guys you were pursuing... pulling me to your chest and forcing your leg between my thighs..."

Recalling the night, Nicole seems distracted while still slowly fisting my pussy. "I know... you weren't feeling well. What does that have to do with... anything?" She almost asks how it relates to my soaking wet sex seizing and clenching on her small hand.

"I had a dildo in my pussy and every time you leaned into me... you were fucking me."

I kept that gem for a special moment, and its impact was even more devastating than I could have anticipated. Suddenly aware of how she looks dressed in lingerie with her hand buried in the pink folds of my sex, Nicole makes an anxious attempt to pull away. I hold her in place with my fingers firmly gripping her forearm. For a minute, she struggles with me. I like to think Nicole succumbed to my lust as soon as she realized how soaking wet my pussy was. In truth, she knows me as well as I know her. Nicole knows this is a setup now.

"You want me to fuck you," she tries to take charge again and I offer encouragement.

"Of course." She can't hide the lust in her eyes, but I pretend I don't notice. "Have you ever fisted a girl before?" She shakes her head. "Not even yourself?" Nicole shakes her head so hard that I'm sure her hair is blurry in the photo that gets taken right at that moment. "So I got your girl fisting cherry?"

Oh, here comes the competitive streak. "Have you?" She asks sweetly, but it's all a cover up.

"Are you offering?" Sucker. I've got Nicole in my crosshairs, and she's not getting away. Not this time. Not when her hand is in my pussy right now.

Her response is cautious, a hint that she's still puzzling over a way out of my trap, and I smile while watching her think it over. "Maybe. With the right person."

Your coaching turns out to be even more useful than I could have anticipated. The words roll off my tongue like gentle kisses. "I have very small hands... Training size even." She can't help looking at my fingers to check for herself. "But I'd..." Here comes the vulnerability Nicole needs to see in order to feel like she is winning. "I'd need you to wear a glove and do my bottom as

"Lust And Dildos 3 (A May Story)"

well..."

The horror of anal! She's totally roped in now, and the sudden eager thrusting motion of her hand within my sex is proof that Nicole isn't going to hold back. "Well, I won't do that. But if you need it to make your boyfriend happy..." I'd laugh if her hand moving in and out of my pussy wasn't already making wet sounds of pleasure. As it is, I'm regretting not setting up a camera to video record Nicole's sudden eagerness to explore my inner depths just to avoid something she can't handle.

|~|~|~|~|~|

May leaned back from her pad of paper and carefully stretched her arms while willing her shoulders to relax. Straddling the soft silicon dildo made it necessary to hunch forward in order to write at the same time. There was a slight knot in her shoulders near the base of her neck, and the way the cushioned dildo spread her buttocks was beginning to ache. With a sigh, she adjusted her posture and closed her eyes for a bit. Her German Shepherd nosed at her bare thigh, content but checking in, and she stroked his broad snout.

There was little point in measuring the toys that Max sent her. That thought made her smile, and May cupped her breasts and gently pinched her nipples. Each dildo was bigger. That seemed to be the deal, and she knew Nicole wouldn't be able to live with that sort of commitment. It was the little texts and encouragement that nudged May along though. The bursts of attentiveness followed by quiet patience. Time enough for her to practice. Time enough for her to write. Time enough for her to explore these pleasures while sharing everything that May wanted to with someone who really cared about her progress and desires.

Another smile and a soft snort. Brute nuzzled her bare thigh again with his moist nose. So long as her desires included steadily fucking her pussy and bottom with big dildos then Max would be interested. May knew she could offer him more than that though. After all, she had an ace in her backpocket.

Corrupting Nicole and bringing her sexy friend along for the ride was totally the sort of thing that would make produce a wolfish smile while Max's sparkling eyes glowed with pride.

"Lust And Dildos 4 (A May Story)"

written by Max D

Featuring May, Nicole, and Max

"Lust And Dildos 4 (A May Story)" themes: MF, D/s, Fingering & Fisting, Vaginal & Anal Penetration, Double Penetration, Stretching, Canine, Implied FF, Strap-On Sex

"Are you insane?" Nicole's chin was trembling while she shook one of my smaller butt plugs at me. "You could really hurt yourself!" Her horror and indignation had nothing to do with protecting me or keeping me safe. "What kind of man would expect you to even use these?"

The way the beige latex plug wobbled in her fingers as my girlfriend repeatedly thrust it into the air between us made me grin like a fool. "A man who knows you couldn't handle anal." I said those words while winking, and Nicole literally dropped my sex toy in shock. It bounced after striking the comforter and then rolled into the crater from the initial impact. "Oh, I think he liked you more than me, but he knew you're too close-minded and judgmental. I'm sorry, sexy. Now what were you doing snooping through my old sex toys?"

"May... I mean... You have more than one drawer?" She was trying to change the topic because I had caught her in the act of spying in my bedroom. This time it would be impossible to claim she was looking for something to wear or innocently putting something away. The fake outrage act vanished, and her eyes darted between me and the plug on my bed as Nicole recognized the extent of her mistake. "He knows me?"

I pointed at my steno pad, still open to the pages my girlfriend had been skimming when I walked in on her, and laughed. "Did you get to the parts of my story where he punishes you for being such a bad friend? You could have asked nicely. I would have told you these things were private, and a good friend would have understood. Of course, if you weren't so judgmental then I would have included you all along. I knew... he knew, too... that you can't handle anything other than plain vanilla hetero sex." She was squirming and starting to get mad, so I pushed her buttons a little harder because Nicole's fury would make it easier for her to take charge while bringing out her competitive streak. "Even though I've always wanted you to be my real girlfriend. You just reject me over and over, so I needed," I gestured toward the beige plug, "to take things into my own hands."

"Lust And Dildos 4 (A May Story)"

Eyes darting around my room, Nicole looked nervous. I had expected her to scream and shout in full tough girl mode, but she was hesitating and that threw me off my game. When she finally spoke up, her voice was weak and uncertain despite the attempt at authority as she made her demands. "Pull off those trousers and bend over, you hussy." I immediately complied, ignoring my girlfriend's obvious moment of weakness, and Nicole rewarded me with a much firmer command as soon as my panty clad bottom was facing her. "These come off, too," she tugged at my waistband. "I want to see what this bulge is... right now."

If Max hadn't coached me, exploring my fantasies about forcing Nicole to submit to me, then I would have panicked. As it was, as soon as her fingers slipped between my blue underwear and my curvy butt cheeks, I was breathing hard and overwhelmed by a hot flash. I couldn't move my hands to my hips to obey her command, and Nicole didn't wait for me. Her fingers took firm grip of my panties, and she pulled them to my knees with a strong tugging motion that stretched the cotton as it passed over my thighs. "Is that what you wanted to see?" I was whispering, my hair covering my face as I turned my head and tried to look behind me, and my girlfriend was petting my ass while perspiration gathered in my cleavage. "How far did you read?" My steno pad had every erotic story that I'd written for Max - in draft form anyway - and it included plenty of dirty details about Nicole inadvertently fucking me while pulling me onto her thigh at clubs so she could attract men.

"Definitely too big for me," her fingers caressed the exposed spread of my buttocks, sizing my anal plug by touch, but my girlfriend still had no idea how enormous the portion inside of me was. "How many times have you tricked me into fucking you?" Her palm was pressing down against the sex toy's base, and I gasped as the very thick soda can sized shaft was thrust deeper into my bottom.

"Twice..." I tried to catch my breath, but Nicole's nails raked over my bare bottom, "three times now..."

Her hand slipped down, between my thighs, and my panties slid down my calves as I shuffled my feet. I was stepping out of them, spreading my legs further apart, as Nicole pushed three fingers directly into my pussy. "Shaved. Exactly the way he likes a cunt. Smooth and wet. So you can fuck better for him." She slipped her pinkie in, accidentally scratching my labia, and cradled the heavy lump of my butt plug in her curled fingers while stroking deep into my pussy. "How many times has he fucked you?" She was getting very personal with her touch, and I knew that Nicole was being too deliberate and was too calm for this to be her first time with a woman.

I needed to know. "Who was she?" I needed to know everything. "When?" Suddenly I

"Lust And Dildos 4 (A May Story)"

understood Max's desire for my stories, my fantasies, and my sexual desires. The heated arousal inspired by my girlfriend's directness was the result of hours spent masturbating while writing out my secret urges. I had seduced myself, shared that passion with him, and I needed so much more because I had imagined so many sexy things.

Nicole blew my mind when she tucked her thumb to her palm and began forcing her hand into my pussy. "I told him that you would do anything he asked." She leaned forward as her thrusts went deeper, my tender opening spread by her thumb joint, and kissed my back through my t-shirt. "I told him you would be a sexy slut if you thought you were hiding it from me." Her fingers pressed past the shallow hollow of my pussy and explored my depths, and the thick plug in my bottom was driven upward into my spine as she closed her hand into a fist. "I told him once you were using big enough toys, once he showed me proof that you were ready, that I'd be willing to fist you every time we were together." I was shaking so hard that my loose pussy was tugging on her arm. "Do you understand?" she whispered to the small of my back. "You could have said 'No' and stopped at any time. You could have resisted his suggestions. You could have..."

My pussy totally betrayed me. A deep passage opened up, eager to be fucked, and Nicole's hand fit into my sex like a key in a lock. I was certain her wrist was a few inches deep, and my smooth labia wrapped around her arm. The pressure of her knuckles and the rocking motion of the plug in my ass pushed me over the edge, and I heaved forward against my bed as I orgasmed on her fist.

My girlfriend didn't stop. She was anticipating my first cum and already seeking out my g-spot while deliberately applying pressure to the base of the thick sex toy in my bottom. "See," she murmured with a smug tone, "the first time you orgasmed on my fist was so easy." She pulled her hand back, and the edge of her pinkie stroked over someplace that felt really good within my pussy. "He told me that, after four or five orgasms, your subconscious will begin directly responding to my fist in your pussy. He said I just need to keep fisting you on and off all night long, forcing your pussy to change its expectations, and then..."

"Then what?" I moaned while feeling a second wave of contractions stirring in my belly. "Then..."

Nicole moved, straightening up and pushing her hand deeper and more directly into my soaking wet sex, and I felt her take control. "And then I can start training you to need my fist, my strap-ons, and my touch to orgasm. Oh, it'll take a while because he spent so much time teaching you how to get off on your own, but he promised me that after ninety days, you wouldn't respond to cocks or even fantasize about men's hands the way you used to." I swallowed, and Nicole laughed. "You know your ass is loose enough to be fisted, too.

"Lust And Dildos 4 (A May Story)"

Not by his big hands... by mine."

She thought that I was anxious because of how she intended to own my pussy and my bottom. The truth was that I knew Max far better than her, and he'd only share me if there was a perverse twist in his plans. "He'll make you pay," I coughed and repeated myself. "He'll make you do something for me." Max never gave away anything for free, but Nicole was too high on her power trip to think things through. "Once you start fisting my ass..."

Taking hold of the butt plug while pressing into my g-spot with her hand, Nicole emphasized her words with hard thrusts that forced me to another orgasm. "You mean when I put both my hands in your cunt? Or you mean when I push one hand into your ass alongside my fist in your pussy? Or you mean when your ass is burning and aching as I stretch it open with eight fingers?" Stroking and lightly pinching my tender vaginal walls, Nicole stole another orgasm from me before the last one seemed to end.

Panting and out of breath, I hoarsely replied, "I'll need it more." It was already true. I could replay every thrust of his sex toys, all the ways they stretched and fucked me, and Nicole's fist was already superior and bold and seeking a fourth orgasm when I would have ordinarily curled up in bed with my Brute pressing his wet nose against my belly.

"No," Nicole serenaded me with a soft shower of coo'ing sounds that barely registered as her hand began moving again. "No, you'll always need it." She helped me understand her plan. "It's what you'll do for it."

When she stopped fucking me and let me catch my breath, I only had one thing on my mind as the persistent buzz of endorphins and bliss overwhelmed most of my thoughts. "What do you want me to do?" I finally whispered as my pussy milked her knuckles. "Will you tell me?" My ass was squeezing down on the soda can shaped anal plug in anticipation of some wicked and perverse demand while my tender and swollen nipples ached with hopefulness.

Nicole rattled off her list of demands like it had been rehearsed over and over. Maybe it was practiced even. Max would have coached her as much as he prepared me after all. "You will use your biggest toys daily. You will provide me with proof each morning and evening that your pussy and ass are loose and open. You will wear whatever I choose in your pussy and ass. You will be stretched until I am satisfied and then you will be pierced. You will only allow men to fuck your throat when you earn the right to have male sex partners." Her fingernails rapped against my bare bottom while I shivered with fresh arousal. "He gets nothing other than stories and photos and videos."

I orgasmed. He'd be so pissed off. I orgasmed so hard that I wet Nicole's forearm with my juices.

"Lust And Dildos 4 (A May Story)"

He'd never be satisfied with just that. I orgasmed so deeply that my lungs ached. He wouldn't accept this without a fight. I started to try to say something, but the words weren't happening. The throbbing and pulsing heat within my belly echoed in my head as my heart drummed against the underside of my breast. "Max..." I managed to sigh.

| ~ | ~ | ~ | ~ | ~ |

He ran his hand over my forehead, soothing my fever, and gently kissed my cheek. The massive plug in my bottom was matched by the realistic latex fist and forearm driven into my pussy. He guided the straw from my drink to my lips, and the rough edge of the plastic was forgotten as soon as the cool sweetened ice tea flooded my parched mouth. "Just another few hours," he murmured, and my pussy clenched down on the fake fist wedged deep within my sex as his fingers drummed over my shoulders. "Do you want to tell me how it feels?"

I'd invited him to visit, to come join me in my home, because I was feeling lonely and unwanted. Masturbating over and over, enjoying the big dildos and sexual urges that I'd come to embrace, I had found myself aroused and empty at the same time. I couldn't tell Nicole, my closest and dearest confidant, anything because it would ruin the heightened pleasure of sneaking around right in front of her eyes. I couldn't ask for a hug, a kiss, or curl up with her even though I desperately needed physical contact. Max came to me, understanding, but he required reciprocation for his support.

Stripped naked, with Brute curled up at the bottom of my bed, I'd offered him all the things that I'd written about. I handed him my steno pad - with drafts of fantasies and torrid affairs that I'd never dared to type up for him. Still dressed, he had sat down and gently massaged and caressed my bare skin. His fingers intertwined with mine, Max slowly explored my erogenous zones with my own hand. All while reading. All while plunging deep into my demented desires and perverse pleasures. All while knowing I needed something more to keep going.

"Like you're making me need it..." I looked over my shoulder and saw my pale body reflected in his glasses. "Why me?" I wanted the answer so badly, but I didn't expect him to say a word.

He surprised me with his tenderness as he encouraged me to roll onto my side and brushed back my hair so I could see him clearly. "Lust is such a lovely thing." Max winked and lifted my hand to his lips and kissed my moist fingers. "I think she'd want to use your biggest dildo as a strap-on, don't you?"

Like that, Max plunged me back into my fantasy. I was the one who helped him tug the massive forearm and fist from my pussy. I was the one who pulled my biggest silicon phallus from under my pillow. I was the one who licked and kissed the head to wet it in preparation while he fit a leather strap-on harness over his trousers and then buckled the sex toy's base

"Lust And Dildos 4 (A May Story)"

into place with a giant steel ring. I was the one who called out her name, "Oooft... fuck... Nicole... harder..." with each of his driven thrusts. I was the one who didn't complain despite how my tailbone was bruised by the large plug in my bottom and how my pussy quickly became tender and sore. I was the one who squeezed down, abs clenching as waves of contractions exhausted me, and orgasmed while being double penetrated. The words he said didn't matter because it was all me.

His touch reminded me that these desires had always been mine, but I wasn't alone.

The next morning, Max was snoring softly on my couch when I tried to walk around my aching pussy and broken ass to get breakfast started. He had tugged off his snug fitting t-shirt but was still dressed otherwise. His small roller bag and heavy backpack were arranged exactly the way he wanted them. His phone was charging where it sat beside his glasses on my living room table. Brute had curled up on the floor next to Max, pushing his back into the couch, and I felt a pang of jealousy over my faithful dog's loyalty to another person.

When he woke, it was like an on button had been pushed, and I watched in awe while eating my granola and yogurt as Max went through a very obvious repetitive sequence as his body and awareness came online. That was the impression I got: "came online" was how it felt, like his breathing was akin to the low hum of electricity charging, and the flexing of muscle and sinew was more mechanical than organic, and I tried to look away but couldn't. When Max focused through the lenses of his glasses, I knew that he saw me. I felt it in my pussy, in my ass, and my heart fluttered while I tried to avoid squirming in my seat. "Did you get some rest?" He was adapting, his neutral fury concealed by a soft smile that didn't match the intensity of his eyes. "A hot bath will help with the soreness. I can run out for a bit if you need more privacy."

Despite the delicate sensation between my inner thighs, I let my legs fall open. I was naked underneath my satin robe, and the cool air sweeping over my warm skin made it clear how exposed my puffy labia were. "You want more?" It was a rhetorical question that didn't require noticing how his fingers subtly flexed while replaying the pleasure of spreading my sex open. "How long are you visiting?" I could tempt him, if I dared, despite my fixation on corrupting my girlfriend with his help.

"How long before this is what you crave and need?" He was smiling, delicately taunting me, but I understood this was a game of cat and mouse. Except, when Max won, he wouldn't simply carry me by the neck to someplace where he could curl up in the sun and enjoy his trophy. "Literally..."

I had an answer, but I swallowed before speaking. My confession seemed surreal given the casual setting in my own apartment with my half finished breakfast on the table in front of me. "It took five times a day for the dildos to be what I fantasized about. Five times a day for the better part of a week. Then I was too sore, too overwhelmed, and too worried to keep going. Except... I spent all my time wondering what it would feel like when I rode them again." Brute lifted his head and sniffed in my direction. He was still sprawled out at Max's feet beside the couch. "Don't give my big boy any ideas, Max. He's very affectionate and looks after me, but not in that way." I had to set some boundaries.

Max just nodded while reaching for his roller bag. "I have something much more reliable for you anyway." He managed to pull his luggage close enough to unzipper it, and took his time fishing out a large black plastic bag that tugged his clothes out with it as it exited his suitcase. "With knots, of course."

I was soaked without even thinking about it. The dildos made a dull thud as they landed on my coffee table, and Brute jumped before nervously settling back down. Max fought the packaging and pulled out three very large sex toys, in dark reds, blues, and greys, and I moaned with my lips pressed together. Each was long and thick - something I knew to expect from him. They had sculpted shafts, artistic glans, and very thick scrotums placed between the middle and bottom of their swollen lengths. "I don't know..." The knots varied from the size of a fist to the size of a softball.

"Vaginally and anally. Five times a day. For one week." He studied me closely, noting how my breathing was racing and my pulse was accelerated. "After that, you can enjoy them when you want."

"You heard what I said..." I was whispering as I

slipped from my seat and knelt on the soft carpet in my dining nook. "You know what that will do to me..." I was weak and leaned forward and crawled toward him on my hands and knees while trying to avoid noticing how much bigger the dildos were getting as I got closer to the coffee table. "You'll have to force me... make me... over and over again..." Max had rules. Only the willing. Only what I could handle on my own. My pussy was so wet that my inner thighs were moist.

He reached out a hand, and I slipped between the couch and coffee table so he could caress my cheek. Brute was right there, smiling while bumping me with his wet nose and wagging his tail, and the immensity of those sex toys was looming beside my shoulder so I forced myself to keep looking straight ahead at Max's lap.

"Yes," he was gentle despite the profound perversity of what he intended. "It's time to force your pussy and ass to go further. After all your hard work, everything you enjoyed last night, you're definitely ready." His fingers brushed my bangs back and stroked across my forehead. "I can stay as long as necessary to make sure the cravings are permanent."

"And Nicole?" I whimpered. I pushed between his legs and rested my head in his lap.

He gestured toward his backpack. "Front pocket, the zip that runs along the side. When you're ready..."

"Lust And Dildos 4 (A May Story)"

I tried to resist, to wallow in the depravity of his comforting touch, but I couldn't contain my curiosity. He watched as I left him, opened his backpack, and then tugged out a leather strap-on harness with raised steel detailing. I turned it over in my hands, examining it, and then looked at Max. The letters on the front panel of the harness spelled out "Nicole," and I knew my girlfriend's name would be stamped into my rounded buttocks or smooth pelvis with every thrust.

"Finish your breakfast, take a long hot bath, and then we begin." He petted my shoulder. "When you're ready."

"Lust And Dildos 5 (A May Story)"

written by Max D

Featuring May, Nicole, and Max

"Lust And Dildos 5 (A May Story)" themes: MF, FF, Dildo Play & Wearing, BDSM, D/s, Strap-On Sex, Stretching, Double Penetration, Vaginal & Anal Penetration, Implied Fisting

"Don't... just... Give me a minute." Nicole frowned as I leaned against the wall in the ladies room and held on tight to my abdomen. "I need to catch my breath."

After canceling plans for three weeks in a row, we'd finally hooked up for a night on the town only to spend most of the evening dealing with mysterious abdominal pain that came in waves every time we danced to a few songs. "This could be serious, May. You haven't even gone to a doctor, have you?" My girlfriend's concern was tempered with frustration. It was impossible to have a good time like this.

"Lust And Dildos 5 (A May Story)"

Shaking my head, I beckoned to my girlfriend to come closer with an outstretched hand. "I'm so sorry," I murmured while focusing on breathing in and out. "It's been a real struggle this month."

Taking firm hold of me, Nicole intended to snap me out of the spell that seemed to have sucked the wind out of my lungs. She couldn't grasp why that wouldn't work. "This could be cysts or worse. If you're in this much pain all month then you need to get it looked at." She frowned as I shook my head. "What? Your secret boy toy got rough? I know you're seeing someone." Frustration became impatience and her fingernails dug into my arms. "Don't deny it."

How much longer I could keep my secrets was unclear. Especially when I was suffering so much for them. "I have a routine," my head slumped to Nicole's chest, and I tried to ignore the flushed heat triggered by brushing against my girlfriend's risqué cleavage. "I didn't know it would take so much out of me."

Strong hands tugged on me until I reluctantly straightened up. "When you tell me then maybe I'll forgive you. You're ruining my night out." Nicole's anger was palpable. Without intending to, I clenched down in response to the fury in my girlfriend's eyes.

Immediately gasping and trembling, I orgasmed with my back sinking into the wall behind me. "Please. Let's not fight. A hug and then... I can wash up and we can dance some more." My legs were unsteady as the buzz of my fifth climax in less than an hour tingled within my toes and fingers. "I should have had a nap or something." I waited for a response, hands palm up and encouraging sympathy, but Nicole was still angry. I was running out of excuses.

Knowing her fingers wouldn't leave a mark, Nicole slapped my face precisely hard enough to indicate she was done playing around but not going to put effort into a fight. "Fine. One hug. Then you get sorted out and I want you by my side. There are at least four eligible men out there who you're putting off. How am I supposed to get laid if you are such a basket case?" She liked how I flinched and tried pulling away from the hug that I'd asked for, so my girlfriend pinned me and held her tight enough for our breasts to rub together. "I know you're not interested in cock lately, but maybe it's time for you to do some swallowing to make it up to me."

Aching as the thick knot within my pussy was gripped tightly by involuntary contractions, I tried to hold on as Nicole's pelvis rocked against the heavy dildo stuffed inside of me. I'd do far more than swallow. The temptation to blurt it out, to tell the truth, was so hard to hold back. "Maybe if it was just you and me," I murmured, but Nicole growled in response. "What would you make me do?" hit closer to the mark while flirting dangerously close to the edge of my unspoken submissive fantasies. "I would..."

"Oh, you!" Nicole stepped backward laughing. "This is all a ploy so you can avoid hooking up with

"Lust And Dildos 5 (A May Story)"

those sexy men." She believed I would never give in so easily without a good reason. "Is one of them an ex? Trying to keep me all to yourself so I can't have him? I'm on to your game." Rolling her eyes and leaving me behind in the bathroom, Nicole tossed a final mocking comment over her shoulder. "I can have whatever I want. You won't stop me, you little slut."

Nearly defeated, I retreated to a stall, carefully pulling out my phone and cupping it in both hands to keep from dropping it, and messaged Max. "I keep cumming. I'm only wearing my small plug but the knot in my pussy feels so good. Every time she touches me... every time she dances with me... I can't control it at all." Sitting allowed my weak legs to relax, but the narrow handle of the two inch thick plug in my bottom dug into my tailbone as the three and a half inch wide bulge of the swollen knot within my pussy pressed on the top of the cone shaped sex toy in my ass. "How do I turn it off, Max? Please. Tell me how."

He'd stayed for two weeks, working from his laptop on my living room table, to make sure I dutifully complied with his instructions. The big dildos he brought were too much at first, the shape of the smooth glans and most of the length sliding easily into my openings but the big knot two-thirds of the way down the shaft bruised my tender pussy and ass instead of going in. Max's strength was amplified by the lusty fantasies he murmured to me as he forced my body to practice and finally broke through my natural resistance. The first knot was only the size of his fist. The last was as big as a softball.

Afterward, hands holding a heating pad to my belly because the deep tissue bruising was too painful to massage away, I sipped coffee with my head in his lap. The caffeine helped with the emptiness within my pelvis, soothed my nerves, and worked better than aspirin for the aches and soreness. My big German Shepherd liked to sprawl out nearby, his wet nose nudging my bare leg now and again, and snore as he napped while watching over me as Brute always had. Max comforted me in my moments of weakness, inspired me with little gifts of dark chocolate, and allowed me a few hours to recover before starting all over again. His tireless attention became a pervasive influence in my home, reminding me of what we expected from my body and sexuality, and I was thankful for how easily he adapted and encouraged my passions.

My fantasies were all about my suspicious girlfriend. The strap-on harness Max brought even had Nicole's name stamped into a metal plate affixed to the leather belt. Every time he thrust deep, with the cold steel pressed against my buttocks or belly, Max asked if I enjoyed feeling Nicole against my skin. The repetition became mesmerizing and triggered latent sensations which lingered along with the pain. Sudden hot flashes came more and more frequently when Max teased me with icy fingertips. Vivid playbacks of imagined scenes from fantasies he'd crafted using my sex journal were triggered every time the supple leather harness was pressed against my bare skin. The thick knots demanded more, and my descent into submission was comforted by an understanding that Nicole would command me to go further. I wasn't even good enough to handle two of the big dildos at a time, but maybe that was intentional so I would be relieved by just wearing my butt plug with the medium or large knotted shaft together. I hadn't cared at the time. I had asked Max to come out knowing he held the key to forcing my body to go beyond what I could do on my own.

I even dared to tell him that.

"No," he replied as my hands trembled in the quiet restroom stall. "This is what you made me work so hard for. You sacrificed so much to achieve this. I don't think you want me to replace it with more." He would know that my pussy was already clenching and on the verge of another orgasm due to the way I read his words in the firm tone which he had used over and over while plunging into me with massive strap-on cocks. "Now go out there and ride her thigh until she either figures out you're stuffed with dildos or you have to call it a night to recover."

Rebellion was something I discovered in the depths of my willingness to submit. "I'll tell her," I hissed while typing the words. "I really well." I knew that it was an empty threat.

He expressed his fury with calculated commands. "I want a story about tonight. It better be good. You woke me from a nap, and you know how much I value my sleep." Nicole would have been aggressive and brutal, but Max wielded rage like a surgeon's scalpel and only cut exactly deep enough to serve his purposes. "How many orgasms?"

Shaking and squeezing my eyes shut, I needed a moment to respond while the shuddering contractions within my pelvis attempted to milk the dildos inside of me. "Seven including this one." I struggled to piece together some measure of self-control, but he'd proven to me that I was mastered by the on-going penetration of my body. "If I write a good story... will you tell me?" I dreaded walking out of the ladies restroom, knowing that my defences were down, and expecting that Nicole would already have a man lined up to fuck me as part of my girlfriend pulling a man for herself.

"Count backward from ten. Touch your fingertips in sequence to your thumb with each number. Linger in the incompleteness, the urge to keep going but you've run out of numbers, and focus on that. That should subdue the craving and urges. Try it now and tell me how it works."

Tucking my phone into my cleavage, I did as he asked. Pointing finger to thumb. Ten. Middle finger to thumb. Nine. Index finger to thumb. Eight. Pinky finger to thumb. Seven. Pointing finger to thumb. Six. Middle finger to thumb. Five. Index finger to thumb. Four. Pinky finger to thumb. Three. Pointing finger to thumb. Two. Middle finger to thumb. One. I paused, wanting to go onward with pressing my index finger to my thumb and almost doing so out of habit, but I was out of numbers. My thumb twitched, waiting, and it seemed so curious that there was nothing more.

"Lust And Dildos 5 (A May Story)"

I repeated the exercise, going faster with familiarity, and it still felt strange despite anticipating the end. Tugging my phone from my bra, I messaged back, "That's odd." I didn't forget the ever present penetration that inspired waves of pleasure and trembling within my sex, but my mind was trying to understand the weird interruption point caused by my finger motions. "Ok. I have to think on that. I will owe you a very good story. Thank you."

"You're welcome."

It wasn't a clean break. My pussy surged with heat as soon as I stood up and pictured Nicole waiting for me. Repeating the countdown, straightening up, I took back enough control to march out of the stall and fix my makeup. My fingers were still moving, stopping, and then restarting when I finally stepped out into the bright lights and music. I had a small passing orgasm when I saw Nicole waiting by the bar with two drinks served in tall cocktail glasses, but I walked it off. The dull throbbing caused by the butt plug and dildo seemed to provide greater clarity instead of plunging me into the feverish fog of my fantasies. It seemed like it was all going to work out.

Until Nicole touched my arm with icy fingers chilled by her frozen margarita with a big laugh. "They have a blender! What a great way to cool you down." I began panting. Max's words echoed in my head while the knot within my pussy shook as I clenched down hard enough to make its long shaft quiver deep within my sex. "The guys left, but let's dance for a bit. The night is ours for the taking!"

Nicole added a little love smack to my cheek, shocking me awake, and leaned in close to add, "Don't ruin my chances again, or we'll be coming out here tomorrow night, too. You owe me."

The first massive orgasm crashed over me, and I was left wallowing in the whimpering aftershocks as my pussy and ass ached for release. "Ok," I muttered while reaching for the bar to steady myself. He was right there, leaning over my shoulder, and reminding me of how good it felt to have Nicole sliding into me. The memories of cold steel pressing against my buttocks as the hefty strap-on dildo popped past my weakening resistance to bury its knot within my pulsating heat were unavoidable. "I can feel it." I was mumbling while pulling the glass closer, trying to get the long straw to my mouth, and Nicole's cold fingers sliding over my arm made me blush as my girlfriend scanned the crowd for cock potential. "I can feel her," I sighed into the plastic straw before sucking hard and flooding my mouth with alcohol and sugar. The cold slush immediately made my head ache as my tongue was frozen, but I didn't care. "I'd do it." My fantasizes took an unexpected leap, and I shuddered as my pussy responded to my perverse inspiration.

Imagining Nicole hammering my pussy with a strap-on as I opened my mouth for his ice slicked cock to push past my lips and into my throat was nearly too much. Only the hard brain freeze was enough to keep me steady as Nicole showered me with commentary about the various dancers and male opportunities over the next forty minutes. It all came to nothing because Nicole was too picky, but the rest of the night was considered a success so I was off the hook until the next weekend. I even got a lift home from my girlfriend without any complaints about being too drunk to walk straight.

Only I understood what was waiting in my apartment. Brute gave my hand a few licks and waited by the bed until I came out of the bathroom. I couldn't sleep until Max had his story. The finger technique bought me some quiet, but the emptiness from having my plug and knot removed was a constant distraction. That inspired me, and my pen began filling pages of my sex journal as it raced to keep up with my imagination.

~~~

The email started with an apology for taking the time to type up and edit the narrative. Max was happy to see anything, but I was upset that he had to wait until after lunch for me to send it. The content made up for the delay, I promised, and he decided to take a break from errands to read the whole story so I'd have feedback. His casual grin as he sat in the Panera with only a bag of chips left from his meal made a few people look his way, but they assumed he was looking at memes on Facebook while he read from his phone.

|~|~|~|~|
~~~

I'm waiting for her to come back. Empty. Hollow. I can feel how my inner walls don't even touch unless I clench down. She's made me so open and left me like this deliberately. If she's gone much longer then I'll have to take things into my own hands, and she knows it. She loves my desperation, loves reminding me of what I need so much, and... I love it, too. There's no longer a question.

I need it.

Her leather strap-on harness is under my pillow so I can wrap my fingers around it as I toss and turn between the sheets. How much longer can I pretend to sleep? How long before crossing my ankles and flexing my thighs isn't enough to distract me? The worst part is the constant tease of my own wetness - not just the slick feeling of my labia sliding over one another as my arousal seeps from the hollow within my pussy, but also the disturbingly erotic grease that spreads between my ass cheeks. She loves that bit the most. Degrading me. Reminding me each time her fingers drag along the line of my spine to my tailbone how far I have gone. Her rough touch disguises how eager she is to force her way into my ass. She only wears latex gloves to emphasize how dirty I am.

Clinging to the supple straps, I know she purposefully puts my sex toys away before leaving me like this. In order to satisfy my urges, I have to get out of bed, cross my room bare naked, and seek them out. Or use my own hands as best I can. Once she knew the truth, that I had grown used to the comforting ache of constantly being stretched and filled by my big butt plugs and huge cock dildos, she made sure I would have to face my craven desires. I would have to crawl on my hands and knees to get what I needed. It was no surprise to her that I would. She chose me to be her friend years ago because I always try to please everyone.

Now I just try to please her. Whatever it takes. And when I fail... when I can't even restrain myself... then her anger is what I deserve.

I'm going to give in. We both know it. It used to be the occasional cruel joking comment. Her hand on my face making me nod my head and agree to her plotting when I was too uncertain to answer a question. Then she realized that a light smack made me pay closer attention. Her fingers striking hard enough to sting but not intended to leave a mark. When she finally found out my secret, discovering I was going out double penetrated with a plug in my bottom and a cock dildo in my pussy, she forgot to hold back. She was nearly incoherent with rage, furious about how I had tricked her into intimacy over and over again by grinding the base of my sex toys against her thigh while she was sexy dancing and luring men to the dance floor, and there was no way to stop her thundering tempest until the storm was done. She stripped me half naked in the empty parking lot, leaving me in my blouse and bra as she ripped my skirt and panties off, and the savage blows of her belt left red welts on my pale thighs while I was humiliated by being bent over the hood of a random car.

The roar of her anger and the lash of her narrow belt continued even when she grabbed me by the arm and dragged me to her car. The crack of leather on my bare skin drove me all the way into the backseat of her Accord, and she didn't stop until her arms grew tired. Still muttering, she shoved my feet the rest of the way into her sedan, closed the door, and came around to the driver's seat. I waited in the silence, knowing the quiet as she drove us out of the lot and headed toward home was just a pause for her to think of more diabolical punishments, and I wasn't disappointed.

"You're going to show me everything you've fucked with your pussy and ass. Everything. I want a front row seat." Her dark eyes seethed in the rear view mirror as she adjusted it to glare at me. "And it better be good."

Her detachment was just another way to manipulate me, but I knew what to expect. When I took out my sex toys, bruises blossoming from the wicked lashes of her belt, she had commanded me to do so completely naked. There was no way to disguise how my labia were swollen and stretched. No way to pretend my ass wasn't still lubed despite excusing myself to wash up. I did my best, arranging my plugs and dildos in size order, and then I waited as she judged them and me while comfortably sitting on my couch.

"Lust And Dildos 5 (A May Story)"

What came next wasn't too surprising. "You're hiding more." She could see right through my reluctance, anticipate the meaning of my uneasy trembling, and called me out. "You show me everything or nothing at all." Her anger was more subdued by far more calculated. "Or would you rather start fucking yourself first?"

My eyes darted toward the small shelves nearby, and her slow nodding indicated I'd given myself away. Brute had been staying by the front door this whole time, but even he seemed uneasy as I dragged my feet across the living room. Shaking, I pulled out my special treasure box, and opened it up.

The leather harness, the one I'm clutching in my fist right now, was the ultimate sin. Confessing to it would mean complete submission to my girlfriend's whims. For a moment, I fought to take back control and deny her what she wanted. That minor rebellion collapsed as I looked over my shoulder and she was already pulling my biggest butt plug toward her. It wasn't about what she wanted. I needed her.

You can't know how hard it was, kneeling in front of her, being told in no uncertain terms what a sex crazed slut I am. Her touch made me stay still, hoping for comfort, but there was none. Her invitation to help her put on the strap-on harness was a chance to make fun of my perverse desires. Her choice of my biggest dildo was meant to humiliate me.

Sitting in her lap, the thick shaft spreading my labia, her fingers pinched my nipples and corrected my posture while her razor sharp words left me exposed and completely vulnerable. I think she expected that I would only be able to handle a few inches at most. Maybe half of the erection. But I dutifully pressed down until the softball sized knot was right against my pelvis bone. It took a moment for her to adjust her expectations and me to reposition myself, but as soon as her hands rested on my collarbone, I knew what she wanted.

"Yes," I murmured. "All the way in."

"What about your ass?" She hated anal. My comfort having my ass fucked was a betrayal which she held against me. "Will it be this easy?"

I closed my eyes and imagined how brutal she would be. A surge of wetness soaked the knot grinding against my opening, and I moaned as my opening stretched in anticipation of the swollen bulb popping into my hollow sex. "If you want it to be." What else could I say? I was hers, completely, as her breasts rubbed against mine while I sank onto that enormous knot.

Shaking her head and then leaning forward to guarantee her whispered rejection was completely clear, my girlfriend replied, "It'll feel like I'm breaking you open every time." She couldn't thrust upward into my pussy, but she could pull on my shoulders to force me onto the big sex toy in her lap. The three and three-quarter inches thick silicon orb was driven past my opening and sunk

"Lust And Dildos 5 (A May Story)"

into my pussy with a sudden rush. I did most of the hard work, but her urging was all the encouragement I needed.

After that, she made it a point to coerce a confession from me while acting as interrogator and lover at the same time. It wasn't until the next morning, when she discovered how easy it was to rip the knot from my pussy and hammer it back in while I was on my hands and knees, that I realized my fantasies were going to come true. My girlfriend's suppressed frustration fueled her libido, and I was on the receiving end of every grudge fucking which she'd never been able to act out in person. Leaving my pussy yawning open and bruised only inspired her to see how far my ass could be pushed next. Our entire weekend was spent proving all the ways I would submit to her lust while she tried to physically break me.

Remembering helps, but now I know exactly what I need. The fist I'm pumping in and out of my ass isn't thick or deep enough to satisfy my urges. It's come down to this, and if I'm going to be punished then it should be for something worthwhile.

Something that turns us both on.

My biggest dildo, with the softball sized knot, is still so difficult to force into my bottom, but I have a butt plug that's even wider at the base. I just need to commit to this, knowing how painful it will be pulling the untapered thickness from my clenching ass, and keep practicing. Eventually the tearing of my puckered anus will break the tight grip of that ring of muscles. Eventually I won't be able to clench down so hard. She'll understand. So long as it's her fucking my ass then that's ok in her book. If I have to give in then she'll want it to be preparation for more.

I'm going to wait for her to come back, but I'm also going to make the most of my time. First by relubing and stretching my ass open. Then by riding my four inch thick plug until I can pop the base in and out without becoming a shuddering wreck. It will take time, but that's one thing I have. It will invite her anger, but she wants the end result.

Even if she can't admit what she needs... I can.

| ~ | ~ | ~ | ~ |

He sent a quick note congratulating me on finally finding my style and voice. What Max left out was how much further I was taking the fantasies which he had entertained about Nicole taking control.

I knew though. I didn't have to be told to understand his genuine praise acknowledged that I was now pursuing passions that were truly mine.

"Lust And Dildos 6 (A May Story)"
written by Max D

Featuring May, Nicole, and Max

"Lust And Dildos 6 (A May Story)" themes: FF, Strap-On Sex, Dildo Play & Wearing, Spanking, D/s, Exhibitionism (Public), Implied MF, Implied Exhibitionism (Video)

"I wish you would be my girlfriend," I grumbled casually while sipping my coffee. "I'm tired of hiding what I want." I was grumpy, irritable, and Nicole's latest rant about conquests and exploits was too much for me to hold back. "Do you care about me at all?"

Nicole rambled on, talking over me again, and then came to a pause when she noticed I wasn't nodding along. "What? I mean... it's funny right?" She looked around, expecting to see something happening nearby, but our usual coffee shop was quiet and mostly empty. "May. Are you feeling alright? Cramps again?"

Asserting myself, I hoped my oblivious crush would get the message the second time. "I said... I wish you would be my girlfriend." Nicole started to object, reeling off all the things we had done together over the past month, and I shook my head and took another sip of my coffee. "In my bed. With me. The way I want." My girlfriend's blank expression said it all. "Are you listening?" My spoon clattered against my cup when I hit the table with my fist. "Do you hear me?"

"Not so... loud," Nicole reached out to me, and the weight of her hand tried to flatten my fist to the table. "Don't cause a scene."

"Like it's not a scene when you trainwreck us into five drunk guys and verbally size up which one you want to take home?" I pushed back from the table, nearly knocking it sideways, abandoned my coffee, and grabbed my shoulder bag. "How many hints do I need to give you? Do I have to spell it out? I'm only in this to spend time with you. For reasons." My cheeks were burning hot and eyes flashed with danger when Nicole tried to reach out and pacify me again. "I'm going home to curl up with Brute. At least he listens to me."

I'm not so proud that I'd hide how badly her rejection hurt. I was crying by the time I got to the sidewalk. All I had wanted to do was explain that it would be really nice to have a proper date, and then I screwed it up. Max had warned me to pick a neutral setting, to be prepared for shock and even rejection, but seeing the look of confusion and terror on my girlfriend's face broke my heart. I couldn't do it. Not anymore. It was a long walk to the nearest bus station, but I needed the time to cool my heels. To think through my next move. To hide my embarrassment.

Chasing after me, shouting my name, Nicole was forced to dodge gawking pedestrians. Early morning shoppers with their push carts and bags stumbled into her path. Men in suits and children in school uniforms swarmed the concrete walkway in front of her. They closed in from all sides as I steadily walked away, head down and tail tucked between my legs, and Nicole almost gave up.

The world intervened. "I'd keep running," an anonymous man in a dark suit muttered to my girlfriend. There was no one there when Nicole wheeled to snarl at him. "Was that why she always kisses you goodnight?" a familiar looking woman asked before stepping into the crosswalk headed the other way. My girlfriend never had a chance to confront her. "She must have been someone special," an old man with a walker shrugged while shuffling past. Voices bubbled up from the crowd, and Nicole was forced to sweep them aside with a flailing arm as her lungs gasped for air. One last sprint, only a block ahead, but the bus was pulling up, and she couldn't see me amongst the people jockeying to get on board.

Fire burning within her chest, Nicole lurched to a stop on the edge of the curb as the light changed and cars pulled ahead right in front of her. Craning her neck, searching for my bright blue blouse in a sea of grey and tan, she took a step back and ran into someone. "Ugh. Sorry." She didn't bother looking. I suspect Nicole thought I was probably right over there, across the street and forty feet away, and there was no way to get to me. Her shoulders slumped, and I saw her acknowledge her failure.

"You chased after me?" My hopeful voice interrupted my determined girlfriend's thoughts. "Did you remember to leave exactly twenty percent tip?" She could be so annoyingly fickle, and I couldn't help needling her.

Exasperated and defeated, she turned to lash out only to discover I was standing right beside her. "Jesus! You gave me a scare. What were you thinking? Why did you leave?" She swallowed hard, sucking air in through her open mouth and flaring nostrils immediately after, and her arms shook as she tried to suppress her emotions. I watched as she struggled to reassert her self control. "How did you sneak up on me?" I shushed my girlfriend with a finger to her lips, and Nicole took several deep breaths. "You can't just storm off like that. It's very rude. We were in the middle of a conversation-"

So that was all. "Oh." Disappointment was written across my face. "Well, if you only came after me to yell at me then I'll be catching the next bus in ten minutes so better make it quick." I didn't need her drama. I didn't want to deal with her criticism.

"No. I mean... May, you can't say things like that in public."

"Lust And Dildos 6 (A May Story)"

Being rejected was bad enough. I should have known Nicole would make me feel even worse given half a chance. "Hello, everyone! This is my now ex-girlfriend! Just thought you would all like to know! These things can't be talked about in public though! It embarrasses her when she makes me cry!" Some people stepped away, others ignored the outburst, and a few pushed in closer to witness the spectacle as I turned back to her with mascara running down my cheeks. "See, you actually can say things like that in public."

"Fuck's sake." Nicole gripped me by the hand and didn't give me much choice while slowly coaxing me out of the crowd and down the sidewalk. "What are you going on about today? What's gotten into you?"

"I want you to be my girlfriend." My girlfriend shook her head like she was trying to escape the very idea of me being serious about my crush on her. "Something you deliberately ignore because you only care about yourself."

"Did someone put you up to this? Is someone putting crazy ideas in your head?"

The whole situation was exactly the way Max had described it. Confronted with something so obvious, Nicole's insecurities made her frustrated and confused. That became anger and irritation. I felt like I finally understood his general disappointment in most people. There was no hope. "Never mind." I wanted to go home and try to forget.

That wasn't enough to imply things were back to normal so Nicole couldn't leave it be. "So you don't want to go finish our coffees?" I shook my head while looking down at where she still held onto my hand. "Maybe hit the cupcake shop." I gave her another head shake. "Look, we can talk about it."

"We are. You're not interested. You use me as bait, flirt with me so men will notice you, and I'm just an accessory for you to dangle on your arm. I get it. I was dumb. I shouldn't have ever let myself fantasize about us. It was all one-sided. All my fault." My tears were silent, but it was impossible for me to hide how much I was shaking.

"You fantasized about us?" Terror wasn't quite the right word for the shock in Nicole's eyes. "You and I... together..."

A flash of fury seized me, and I yanked my hand from her grip. I had to literally push her out of the way, and then I started to head in the direction of the open market. "Yes. Don't remind me. I was such an idiot." Again, Nicole reached out and tried to restrain me, but I tugged free of the fingers that grabbed at my shoulder. I couldn't stop Nicole from following though. "Leave me alone. I'm going to do my shopping."

"I always enjoyed kissing you."

As one, we stopped on the sidewalk. "What?"

"I'm serious. You're the best kisser." I turned to face my girlfriend, and Nicole was staring down at her shoes. "I've always thought you're better looking than me, too. Atrocious fashion sense," she quickly caveated her statement, "but without you, men wouldn't even know I exist."

"So I'm an accessory wearing bad outfits? You really know how to make a girl feel like a million bucks."

Closing the distance, pulling me into her arms, Nicole kissed me like she meant it. Crushing my breasts, tonguing my lips, she lingered and explored the heartfelt willingness within my trembling embrace. We didn't fit together perfectly, there was a sense of physical awkwardness, but the emotions were real. "Best kisser bar none," she murmured as my breath tickled and warmed her upper lip. "What... did you have in mind?"

It was too much. I couldn't tell what was real and what was manipulation. Eyes squeezed shut and still silently weeping, my voice broke when I replied, "Everything." Despite the tangible reality of my crush's heart beating fast against my breast, Nicole's flushed heat warming my skin, and the arms wrapped around her... I was convinced this was a setup. How could I love someone so cruel? How could I be such a fool?

"I don't have any... I've never done that before."

Sniffling, I contradicted my girlfriend. "You've fucked me to orgasm so many times on the dance floor. You just didn't notice. You were too busy chasing boys."

Kissing my delicate lips, Nicole did her best to be kind despite her natural defense mechanisms filling her head with sarcastic suggestions. "I knew the cramps were from dildos, dummy. I knew you were grinding them against my thigh to get off. I'm not stupid. I figured you were experimenting and pretended not to know so you wouldn't be embarrassed." She kissed me again. "I don't know how to even... Like how is it supposed to work? With guys, you know, they just whip it out and stick it in and, bam, they're done. It's pretty damn simple."

Maybe it could be real. "Tell me," I whispered quietly, "what I should fuck for you. It's that easy." I took a slow breath and exhaled it to Nicole's lips. "Kiss me. Hold my hand. Touch me." I was clinging onto a sliver of hope that my crush wasn't deliberately toying with my emotions. "Command me."

"Oh, shit," my girlfriend moaned. "You've been checking my damn browser history. You sneaky..." She swallowed her accusation when it was obvious that I didn't understand while looking into her eyes. "So just because I'm turned on by watching dommes put bitches in restraints and fuck the hell out of them doesn't mean I have any idea how to do that." The red glow of my blushing cheeks made her sigh. "Is that what you want? I mean... Would you really do that?"

"Would you?" In my mind, I was paralyzed by the idea that Nicole might be into exactly the sort of dominance and submission which terrified and turned me on.

"Lust And Dildos 6 (A May Story)"

Quietly kissing me again, Nicole took control. "My girlfriend. Ok. Fine. I have expectations." I couldn't help shivering in anticipation. "First, we are going to finish fresh coffees. Then, grocery shopping." She watched how delaying the inevitable stirred dizzying passions between my erratic breaths. "And, once we're back at your house, I expect you to show me everything."

"Really?" I was giving her too much control, and that made my heart leap with anxiety. At the same time... isn't this what I wanted?

Running her fingers over my cheek, letting her fingernails lightly claw at my pale skin, Nicole fell into her typical casual pattern of dominating me with an added twist of arousal. "Yeah. You're going to fuck everything for me today." She forced her tongue into my pretty submissive mouth, enjoying how there was no resistance to her demands, and smiled. "Would you like that? Being my slut? Is that what you were so upset about? Should I force you to get down on your knees and suck my pussy while you're wearing a plug?" The trembling panic that swept over me inspired my would be domme's dark fantasies, and Nicole didn't hold back much. "I get so wet watching sluts crying while getting hammered by dildos and cocks. I love how they drool all over their tits while they're gagged and locked into restraints. And," she nipped my earlobe while savouring how I whimpered with lust, "the way their pussies hang open, the bruises and whip marks on their belly and breasts, and the steel speculums pulling their asses apart..."

Gasping, I was on the verge of cumming from Nicole's voice alone. "All of that," I pleaded. "Please. Make me. Don't stop." I was desperate for more but didn't know how to ask for it.

"I don't believe you," Nicole said matter of factly. "You're trying to impress me or something, aren't you?" I shook my head, vigorously rejecting any assertion of falsehood, and my girlfriend swooped in for the kill. "Finger yourself. Cum for me. Right now. No one's watching. Prove it."

Staring into my girlfriend's eyes while shaking with adrenaline, I reached down and slid a hand between my trousers and top. My fingers were cold, chilling my warm skin, and I had to push around the folds of my tucked blouse to slip them into my panties. With Nicole hugging me, I explored my tingling arousal, sought out my smooth labia and swollen clit while slumping forward, and blinked while actively fondling my sex. In public. On a sidewalk in the morning light. With the cool kiss of a whispering breeze tickling the perspiration on the back of my neck. Because I was commanded to do so.

Sensing my weakness while in awe of my submission, Nicole whispered, "What do you really fantasize about?" She needed to know before sharing any more of her own secrets.

"You," I swallowed while the feverish glow at my fingertips became waves of contractions. "You with a strap-on." It was going to happen. Somehow, I was going to get what I deserved. "I... More but..."

"Lust And Dildos 6 (A May Story)"

"But you didn't want to ruin the real thing? How sweet." Nicole delicately kissed me, nudging me so we were less exposed as some people walked by, and smiled. "I've always wanted your head between my thighs, licking my pussy, since you're such a good kisser. I've always wanted to know, since you are such a cockblock, how well you fuck your toys. I've always wanted to see you in action. Wondered about us having threesomes with a guy. Wanted to watch you suck him off." Every word was thrust into me, and I wobbled within my lover's hug. "We can start with a strap-on. I'll want a lot more though."

Clenching as the growing hunger within my pussy threatened to set off a climatic explosion, I swallowed and murmured, "Fisting me, too." My knees gave out, and I leaned against my girlfriend's chest when I saw Nicole's devious grin. "However you want to," I sighed while listening to the steady rhythm of her heat against my ear.

"Such a naughty mess." With two kisses and a smack on my bottom, Nicole helped me straighten up. "We need a bathroom stop so you can wash yourself." Without really thinking it through, as soon as my hand escaped my trousers, she lifted my fingers to my mouth. "Lick them clean at least. I hope you like the taste of pussy."

I was flushed and overheating, overcome by the sexual possibilities which beckoned in my lover's smile, and I did as I was told. Happy and docile, I followed Nicole to the market restrooms on unsteady legs. We had fresh coffees, got groceries together, and I got a ride home from my girlfriend. It seemed like a fluke, like my imagination had gone wild, but, when the door to my apartment closed, Nicole took over again.

"While you put away everything, where is your toy collection?" Ordinarily, she'd have checked the drawers on her own. Sneaking around didn't seem to be necessary if I was serious about being her slut.

"Under my pillow, in my lingerie drawer, and..." Nicole didn't back down despite my hesitant blushing. "And the strap-on harness is in the gift box on the shelves beside the couch."

"Something I should know?" my girlfriend asked while heading there first. "Will I be disappointed?"

"Ummm..."

It was leather and clearly handcrafted. The workmanship was top notch. Nicole turned it over in her hand, stared at it, and turned to glare at me. "It has my name embossed on it." She looked back at the harness, checked for anything else, and then noticed his mark. "Oh, fuck. What have you promised Max? You know he's insane."

"Stop complaining," my defensiveness caught us both by surprise. "When I told him I was fantasizing about you, he didn't even try to take advantage or change that. Consider yourself lucky." I pulled the fridge door open a little too fast and rattled the bottles on the shelves. "Unless you'd prefer I be his slut instead of yours."

"Lust And Dildos 6 (A May Story)"

The silence that followed lingered between us for several breaths. "I definitely prefer you being my slut." Nicole set the harness down. "Do you want help putting things away?" I couldn't be sure of anything. Either this was for real, or I was having one hell of a wet dream.

Acknowledging my uncertainty but reframing it as a positive, I posed with one hand lifting my breasts up to push my cleavage into view. "Yes, and... while you help... you can tell me how I can be a good slut for you."

We eventually ended up in my bed. My toys were scattered across my dresser, bedside table, and by my pillows. The lube bottle was tipped over on a towel, rocking with the motion of the mattress, while my breasts swung back and forth from hard thrusts that battered the back of my thighs. Submission came easily when I had spent so long imagining Nicole's demands. Words were kept to a minimum, each of us silently seeking to be good at something missing, and the mechanical had overcome the attraction and arousal of the moment. Brute whined occasionally on the other side of the closed door.

Our first time was awkward and strange, and neither of us felt comfortable no matter how often we changed positions. Nicole's curses matched my frustration after another attempt at doggy style sex. "I'm just going to fucking call him. Seriously. Why the hell won't this harness stay in place?" Nicole tugged at the waistband, flinched as the base of the dildo dug into her pelvis, and growled bitterly when the weight of the silicon cock made the front leather panel pull away from her skin. "Was it this difficult when he was wearing it?"

Bruised and sore, I offered an alternative. "Why don't I ride it for you? You can watch, and we'll fix the harness later." I really wanted to orgasm, but something went wrong every time I got close. "He had a lot of practice. Maybe it just doesn't fit right."

The percussive smack of Nicole's palm battering my bare ass cheek echoed in the bedroom. "My slut! Not his!" I suspected her hand ached as she drew it back, but the red blemish on my skin seduced her rage. "Can you cum from being spanked while rocking onto my big cock? What would it take?" The dildo shuddered from the motion of my girlfriend's hips as Nicole slapped my milky white buttocks over and over. "I need a leather paddle. A wooden one with studs. Can you even feel me?" She tried to shake off the pain, but even her fingers were sore from bouncing off my hard bottom. "I'm going to leave welts on your pretty ass!"

It didn't feel very sexy in my head, and I had to brush aside distracting thoughts. I could admit that my pussy was definitely warming up. I could accept this was new for both of us. I just wanted it to be better already. "I..." I didn't want to ruin it. I took a deep breath, closed my eyes, and embraced a new appreciation for the way Max had always kept his emotions separate from his actions. "Make sure the bruises are even," I suggested meekly. My lover would need to be coached, to be encouraged, and to learn my body in ways that he had understood without asking. "I'll want to remember." His competence was something I had taken for granted. "I'll want to see them darken and turn colours in the mirror all week." I shuddered when fingernails raked over my lower back, and I whispered, "You'll want to practice..." Max hadn't needed practice. He had been there, in my living room and my bed, to teach me so I could educate Nicole.

That epiphany evoked calm and stillness despite the amateurish spanking and insecurity motivating Nicole's urge to leave me marked. "Don't tell me what to do! I know-"

"You don't though," I shaped the words with effortless calm. "We need to practice. We need to figure it out." I slipped forward, escaping the silicon shaft partially thrust into my pussy, and turned over while smiling at my girlfriend's scowl. "Look at you," I blew Nicole a kiss. "So angry. So hungry. So... beautiful." I closed my eyes, already knowing the fury which would crease my lover's forehead without needing to see it, and wondered if Max had been coaching me all along to make this night less of a disaster. "I'm your slut now. You've seen all my toys... and we've not even talked about all the ways I enjoy fucking myself." With a deep breath, I took the plunge hoping my girlfriend's anger wasn't the end of us both, "I know you will be so good at fucking me that I'll never even fantasize about someone else."

Irritated by the dangling strap-on cock but not able to toss it aside without fumbling with the buckles snugging the harness to her hips, Nicole moved closer on her knees and then collapsed onto the bed beside my naked body. The wet silicon cock splatted against my thigh, and we both looked down and rolled our eyes with a laugh. "You really fantasized about... this?" She had been beaten by a damn leather harness, by the way the weird dildo kept bobbing up and down unless she kept a hand on it, and it was unnerving to realize this was something she had no idea how to do well. "It looks a lot easier in videos."

Running my hand over Nicole's thigh, I murmured, "You are so demanding. Ok. I'll do it." I chuckled peacefully when Nicole lightly smacked my bare breast. "But remember, it was your idea to make videos for Max. You made me do it."

Eyes opening wide, Nicole tugged on my shoulder to turn me on my side so we were facing each other. "What? I didn't make you do any such thing. My slut. My-"

"Prove it to him. Show off how much better you are. At fucking me. At commanding me. At dominating me. At making me your slut." I winked. "Can you imagine how furious he will be?"

The glittering within Nicole's eyes made it clear that defeat had been transformed into opportunity. "You are going to blow him away," my lover assured me with an evil grin. "Oh... better than that..."

"Hmmm?"

"We'll invite him to visit and put on a show."

Pussy gushing from an instantaneous orgasm, I

"Lust And Dildos 6 (A May Story)"

swallowed hard and nodded. "You'd make me... perform for you and him?" I knew that my lover had no idea how much submission that would require nor how much it turned me on.

Lazily tweaking my trembling breast, Nicole shrugged. "You'll fuck in front of him like a pro." Settling back into the pillows while picturing how Max would try and hide his interest and affection, she grinned and added, "A nice leather collar would look good on you. Plus I could hold onto your neck easier to pull you into my thrusts."

Swooning while listening to my girlfriend's inspired breathing, I embraced my passions and hoped for the best.

Cherish Desire Creators

Our Creators

Cherish Desire works with amazing skilled and experienced writers, editors, narrators, video narrators, models, photographers, musicians, and muses to create written, audio, and video content along with the supporting graphics, trailers, and music clips. While Max tackles the majority of assembling their contributions into a finished format, Cherish Desire would be a lot less without their involvement.

Max

Max is always watching except when he chooses to look the other way. He's the go to guy for those crazy sex situations that a man – especially a very straight man – shouldn't be so knowledgeable or insightful about. He "just knows that stuff." When not receiving messages and snaps from his sexy ladies, plotting his itinerary to swing by Hamburg, Ipswich, Wien, Linz, or Wiesbaden, and not lowkey terrorizing the West Coast by simply showing up and doing as he likes, Max stays close to his home office hidden within the suburban sprawl near an international airport. He is distinctly unsupervised though there are plenty of demands on his time. The Empress and Goddess, along with a few others, keep an eye on him locally. Various teams and squads are often close by at festivals and events. None of that really keeps him in check though. Max is an unrestrainable phenomena with more in common with a hurricane than humanity.

That's the official blurb anyway. Here's a little bit more since you've read this far.

He was talking through innumerable drafts, hundreds of thousands of words now hammered out and crafted with the fancy DAREU LED mechanical keyboards that he upgraded to while trying to cope with the pandemic shutting down all travel, and Max paused with a frustrated growl. "Another pain cycle." There is no relief for it, only prevention and a different pillow, because the tension in his mood has translated to muscles pinching nerves running into his jaw. In thirty minutes or so, it'll pass more or less. He resumes talking, irritated, and explains he has no idea what to do with all the things still unwritten. Lelith and the Wulf Daughter aren't going to take it on. The Unicorn will be left with an encrypted hard drive when she sorts through his belongings. With digital, there is no "lost manuscript" found decades later.

The laughing must hurt, but he laughs anyway. "One last print job…" If this is how we die, found collapsed at home, will there be an out of paper light blinking on his laser printer because he decided to dump twenty megabytes of TXT files to paper? Max moves on but the question lingers. How permanent is any of this? Is that the purpose now?

We met a long time ago now. He would have been in his early thirties if I do the math. I was younger than that, doing my thing which usually involves stage work, performances, promotion, event management, and coddling egos. I doubt I was the first Valkyrie he took an interest in. His taste in women swings wildly between pixies, witches, cultists, wild women, and powerful hitters like myself. His ridiculous crushes on musicians… but I digress. I was doing my own thing. Our paths crossed.

This was back in the days of LiveJournal and CorpGoth. Back when he first started coming out to live shows after a long time spent avoiding unpredictable crowds. He mostly danced. By himself. Listening to the music. Clearly enjoying it – whether the bands or DJs were playing – and that made him singular even within an eclectic crowd. Many years later, Max confided that he had no idea how to dance with people anyway. "It's all just martial arts shifted, transformed, and shaped to serve a purpose." I asked him what that meant. "They are so busy watching me, making fun of or playing along, that in order for someone to assault me, they have to step right into that spotlight." He was deadly serious. "Most casual predators aren't going to risk that. Not without being very drunk or high, without being egged on by their boys, or without some posturing and bellowing. By then, I've already decided on how it ends. How they end." His satisfied smile, low chuckle, and comfortable body language sum up a lifetime spent behind enemy lines, besieged by humans, and how easily he can accept violence as a solution.

Our paths crossed again. He remembered me. Said hello. I'm a pretty good judge of attraction, but we don't have the "let's get naked" chemistry. His honesty is unsettling. I can't really think of many people who have nothing to lose being themselves so openly, but I suppose Max figures that people are going to attack him just for existing so why hide. We have conversations that are half therapy, half madness, and half inspiration. We started meeting for drinks whenever we were in the same city. His Sprite. My whatever would help me pass out for the night.

Then there was a long interval of, well, nothing. He had slowly and deliberately pruned entire networks of people from his life. I don't think any of us really noticed or thought much about it. How easy it was for him to be present, choose his time, and exit. We are so stuck in lingering forever with the same people and trying to collect more that the idea of letting go only comes with scary considerations of mortality. For Max, it was natural. He'd always been one ambush away from the dying on his own. He had too much to do to maintain people who never grew, evolved, and became more.

Independent Bar. iBar for short. Downtown Orlando which is hardly a downtown at all by city standards. My reluctant beau and I venturing out for a laugh, drinks, and some good music. Ok. My Florida beau is a privileged man-pet who doesn't deal well in public, but I wanted to get out of his house and do something so he humoured me. I suppose he saw me first, saw I was with a boyfriend, and left it at that. In hindsight, he'd come close twice, but I'd not put the pieces together. Not until I saw him dancing. Not until he was hanging close to the bar with a tall angular woman, and then I realized what I was seeing.

Max. Everyone makes up images of people they talk to but don't see. Of what musicians and movie stars look like off camera. Of what an author or voice on the radio might look like. We were all aging, and he was no different, but it didn't seem unusual at roughly annual intervals. This time…

He'll say that he has gone too far. That each trip across the Atlantic ripped him further from the fabric of what everyone else experiences. That his evolution was likely inevitable. As Devourer. Into the Abyss. As Wulf, Monster, or whatever else is easiest to disarm people who want to pin him in place. Eating outdoors at the Irish Pub in Disney Springs, we talk about things which could just be superficial chitchat, but he layers meaning within breaths and words with an uncanny directness. And none of that makes him sending me Bad Dragon toys and laughing about my indecision over what I want from him any easier.

From one Bunny to the world, this is all about choice. Beware of where choices lead you, or throw yourself into the maelstrom. It may be the exact same outcome anyway. You can't go back, don't get an undo, and you have to be ok with that, too. Some decisions change everything.

You made one picking this up, reading it, and coming this far.

Maybe your choices will change everything.

Cherish Desire Erotica

Very Dirty Stories

We wanted to share our favorite sex stories. The ones that broke out of the conventional erotica mold, shattered the limitations of casual romance and sex, and dove into detailed and realistic action involving stretching, large sex toy play, vaginal and anal fisting, domination, fantasy monster and animal dildo play, restraints and suspension, elaborate medical and DIY devices, and more. We did it bit by bit, discovering and learning as we went, and released volume after volume of two to five short stories to challenge readers to be sexually aroused by something truly intense or charmingly subtle. Very Dirty Stories volumes are about ladies that expose themselves and embrace their fears and desires as well as the men and women that inspire them to sexual peaks while living out wild sexual fantasies.

Singles

We wanted to publish sexual adventures that were more than a one night stand. So we gathered together our favorite ladies and delightfully sexy themes and created Singles - longer collections of sexual stories that fit together to cover formative physical and psychological experiences that define her womanhood or establish a collection of deviant delights and sexual alternatives. These trailblazing erotica books go deeper, harder, faster, and expose the soft white underbelly of sensual need while delivering thrust after thrust of sexual intensity and the soothing pleasures of passionate affection. Explore the explicit erogenous zones of women and their sexual partners. Be prepared for sexually challenging situations as well as character details that get beyond height, weight, hair colour, and favorite size of dildo. Plunge into their stories and get wet. Singles also make great gifts for that secret someone who needs a sexual swift kick in the nuts or a perverse surprise stashed for long trips and evenings in.

~~Very~~ Wicked Dirty Stories

The darkness of desires are shadows always encircling the hope of fulfillment and pleasure. These are the twisted realities fueled by the uninhibited passions and believes of the few. Their sexual urges, their powerful alliances, and their willingness to defend their own as well as to strike out and forcefully embrace what they require. ~~Very~~ Wicked Dirty Stories hint at the unobserved and strange frayed edges of reality that we like to censor or ignore. Ghosts, shapeshifters, and great powers linger just beyond the firelight while watching humanity sleep.

Divinations

Cherish Desire Divinations erotica delves into darkness. Lusty shapeshifters, impassioned spirits, dangerous players, and perverse pagan deities beckon with sordid promises and unseemly urges. Their intense passions expose their bestial and heavenly natures while emphasizing how closely they represent unfettered hunger, cunning, love, and wickedness. Divinations was born of fevered imaginations and sexual abandonment that left us aching, bruised, and hoping for more. Divination books are collections of erotic stories that go deep and explore psycho-sexuality as well as physical modifications suited to the nearly immortal. The limited disguise of humanity has been stripped away, and the results are animalistic sexual rituals and self-enlightened spirituality that arouse jaded desires for more.

Cherish Desire apologizes in advance for exposing the true nature of shapeshifters and the transcendent hungers that lurk behind every door and under every bed.

Discover More

For our complete catalog of titles, explore our books: https://wulf.fun/CherishDesireErotica

For more about your favorite characters, check out the ladies: https://wulf.fun/CherishDesireLadies

Very Dirty Stories, ~~Very~~ Wicked Dirty Stories, Cherish Desire Singles, and Cherish Desire Divinations titles include over 450 erotica stories to delight even the most jaded readers. With a focus on perverse desires that push limits to achieve blissful pleasure, intense action and taboo desires inspire fantasies and arousal for a satisfying climax.

The majority of Cherish Desire titles are available in digital editions with audio, video narration, and paperback editions for select stories and books.

And when you visit the Cherish Desire Catalog, get elite and a free eBook from Cherish Desire by signing up for the inside track.